CW00551004

די ווילדע צילקע

ISBN 9791096677115

An earlier version of this translation first appeared in *In Geveb: A Journal of Yiddish Studies*, serialized between Jan–May 2021.

ZUSMAN SEGALOVITSH
Tsilke the Wild

Translated from the Yiddish by Daniel Kennedy

Farlag Press

1
Tsilke and Aunt Nikhe

A LARGE FOREST.

All around woodlands, vast and thick, extend in every direction, trees swaying silently and pensively in the wind.

Now and then, the dark shadows split and the sky mixes with the earth, the earth with the sky.

Roads, rivers and streams snake through the woods.

Here and there, lumberjacks fell the largest trees, leaving behind a graveyard of roots.

But leaving the vast woods for a moment to their noise—we lose our gaze in the green shadows, and we listen . . .

A narrow stream meanders through the pine-forest; its water, reflecting the canopy above, appears smooth and green.

The stream is curbed in places by old branches, rocks, and logs. The water flows back and forth, rushing and shouting, babbling in its aquatic tongue. The trill of a bird, the squeaking of a squirrel—the rare tones of nature.

Day and night pass here in tranquility. Ants in their millions creep along the ground, dark dots scurrying in every direction; they too are in league with the earth, a part of the whole.

But what do the ants matter? Entire species have vanished—giant animals—mammoths—turned to ash and dust. Mighty cities have been laid waste. The pyramids in Egypt are crumbling . . .

And yet here, ants creep upon the earth, little dots . . . what do they matter?

One day, a tree will fall, and there will be no trace left of a million such living grains of sand.

But for now, every breath of the forest lives for itself and by itself, reticent and mute. Hushed shadows. A spot lights up, having snagged some sparse rays of stolen light. When did it begin, the silence of the eternal, and when will it end?

But there's one corner of the forest where life is a little different.

Here we find a trio of cabins and some stables. There are clothes drying on a washing-line hung between two trees: white shirts, blue and red quilt-covers and dresses, their colors—a sudden break in the surrounding green.

There's a cart without a horse, a few broken chairs and various household utensils lying around by one of the doors.

It's quiet all around.

The windows of one of the cabins are wide open, but there is no other sign of life.

The two other cabins are closed up on all sides, by all appearances empty.

A passerby might assume that this is an abandoned forest settlement. But if one listens, one will hear a rhythmic slopping sound coming from the direction of the river; someone is washing clothes there where the stream is narrow and the water flows faster.

A woman in her fifties sits, hunched over, washing one piece of clothing after another.

She is completely drenched, a few gray hairs creeping out of her headscarf. She looks into the water and, noticing her reflection, tucks the loose strands back under her headscarf.

For a moment she pauses in her work, listening out for something, peering between the trees; she calls out:

"Tsilke, Tsilke!"

She calls the name twice, and both times the forest answers with an echo:

"*Tsil—ke, Tsil—ke!*"

But the real Tsilke does not respond. The old woman returns to her work, thrusting the laundry into the water—splish-splash.

A pinecone comes loose from a tree above and falls into the river with a plop, it starts to drift, disappearing swiftly with the current.

The old woman pauses occasionally, while the water rushes past, reluctant to rest for even a moment as though, through its terrible haste, it hopes to embarrass the large, green trees, which stand forever frozen in place, in duet with the squeaking of the squirrels.

You should be ashamed of yourself, ancient, mighty forest! I'm just a narrow stream and I've already traveled all over the world, while you were born here, and will die here. Shame on you, forest!

So it goes: the droning lull and the monotonous tumult.

Suddenly, from another part of the woods, the sound of singing can be heard:

> "*Reyzke sees through the window*
> *That Esterke's sad and listless,*
> *What's the matter Esterke?*
> *My lover has a mistress.*"

It's the voice of a girl. That last line is picked up by the echo and carried far across the trees: "*My lover has a mistress.*"

The old washer-woman lifts her head and calls out:

"Tsilke, Tsilke, would you ever come over here!"

"I'm coming!"

Tsilke springs out from behind the trees. Barefoot, in a light little red dress, she leaps over the stream and approaches the old woman.

"Come on then, help me hang up this washing," the old woman grumbles.

"Are you angry, Aunt Nikhe?" Tsilke asks and, without waiting for an answer, begins gathering the wet laundry in her arms and goes over to the washing line, which hangs from a tree, speaking to herself as she does so.

"Aunt Nikhe is angry, father is angry, Shleyme the clerk is angry, everyone is angry, everyone is busy and bad tempered."

She lets out a sigh, and starts to sing again:

> *"Reyzke tries to comfort her*
> *Ester cries more than she reckoned*
> *Wait down by the gate,*
> *I'll be there in a second."*

Then, having hung up the last of the washing, she approaches the bank of the stream and starts splashing her feet in the water. She kicks hard with a sudden, unexpected temper, as if the water itself had done something to deserve it.

She has a round face and blonde hair, with grayish eyes under brown eyebrows. And though outwardly her face conveys volatile indignation, around her lips there are signs of a stifled smile beneath the surface.

She is nineteen, but there is something about her more redolent of a sixteen-year-old; she is clearly still up for all kinds of mischief.

Aunt Nikhe has finished her task and asks, "Where were you, Tsilke?"

"At the distillery; I was looking for Shleyme. He's heading into the city and I wanted to send a letter."

"Who would you be writing to?" the old woman pried. "To *him*?"

"To *him*, to *him*," Tsilke mimics her aunt, kicking the water and sending a whole cascade of spray splashing into the air.

"He hasn't forgotten you yet then, that Sasha, no? There aren't enough girls for him in the big city, I suppose?"

"He says he would gladly give up half the city for one single smile from me. Tell me though, I don't understand why he wants my smile so much."

"You're naive still. He likes you—and if he likes you, he'll take anything you have to give."

"Aunt Nikhe, last time he was here he said that, if I wanted, he'd take me with him to the city and never leave me."

"You silly thing."

"Well what do you think he comes here for then? You think he's interested in his father's business? They could raze the entire forest to the ground, or leave every tree standing, it would make no difference to him. He comes because of me."

"Foolish child. And what do you think his father is going to say, a rich man like that? What are his family going to say? You think they'll let him marry the daughter of a forest warden? Let it go, foolish child, come inside, it's time to make dinner. Your father and Shleyme will be back from the distillery soon."

The two women walk away from the stream; around them the forest sings its quiet refrain, while the stream continues to murmur.

Tsilke is deep in thought, but suddenly she resumes her song:

> *"Comb your hair and dry your tears,*
> *before your lover overhears . . ."*

With these last words she runs into the house, and the red of her little dress vanishes from the green backdrop of the woods.

All is quiet.

There isn't another living soul for miles around. The trees stretch upwards to the sky, and the forest is left alone to its own devices.

But someday soon the water from the stream will stop, and the trees will stretch out on the earth, like a flock of drowsy, well-fed sheep.

Without warning the cry of a squirrel, a wild, cat-like sound, cuts through the silence and a little later, it's joined by the call of the cuckoo. The woods are alive, alive without people, or fanfare.

No wind stirs, and the sun bores through in places, singeing the trees.

Here and there, golden droplets of resin, transparent amber, begin to flow.

A pine cone, fresh and ripe, drops from a tree and lands on the earth with a thud.

The melodious silence continues until Tsilke starts singing again, and music pours out through the open window:

> *"Reyzke goes out walking,*
> *Ester comes to see,*
> *You're such a pretty girl,*
> *Would t'were true of me."*

Aunt Nikhe walks around adjusting the washing lines. Hearing Tsilke's song, she glances in the direction of the house, shakes her head and lets out a sigh. It's not clear whether she is angry or concerned.

Out here in the forest, surrounded by quiet, lonely people, Tsilke has grown up to be peculiar. Nikhe is not her
real aunt, but a distant relative, taken on by Tsilke's father
to look after Tsilke following his wife's death when Tsilke
was just a baby. Aunt Nikhe took over the running of the
house.

She was a widow, without children of her own and
without a home. Tsilke was her sole consolation and had
become her whole life. Nikhe suffered terribly that time
when Tsilke was sent away to school in Grodno.

The only thing she had left then was her book of Yiddish
Bible stories. On Shabbes, when the forest was quiet, she
would drape a shawl over her shoulders—no matter the
temperature, she always wore her Turkish shawl—and
open up the book, she would sit by the window, reading
until darkness fell. And when she came to the story of
Rachel and Leah, she would shed tears while the forest
sang along.

Iser the forest warden was a man of few words. He had
been very fond of his late wife, and he seems to go around
now with an unspoken rage against God for having tak-
en her away from him. He knew a little Torah and was so
honest that one could trust him with any sum of money.

Yet he seemed to harbor doubts about God's sense of justice.

Iser traveled through the forests with a grubby little notebook where he would jot down calculations for his employer, the lumber merchant Lurie. In Grodno the Luries had a large office staffed by many servants and accountants, but Iser did things more simply; his entire office fit snugly inside his notebook.

Business was booming. They exported abroad. Germans came down as far as the forests and the tight-lipped Iser explained everything to them in his broken German.

But people had the impression that Iser had his own preoccupations, that the whole business with the Luries and the Germans was just a side project.

On Shabbes he would read a holy book, or go for a stroll in the woods.

He seldom left the forest when Tsilke was at home. But in the days when Tsilke was away in Grodno, he would go to Mistebove, to Shmuel the leaseholder in Prudne, and spend Shabbes there. Nikhe would stay behind, alone in the forest with her Torah. She felt very lonely, but sometimes she'd look up from her book and gaze out into the verdant woods and her soul seemed to sing—for God spent Shabbes in the forest. Every bend of a branch, every rustle of a blade of grass, was holy. The forest was enveloped in beams of light, cradled in sacred noises.

There was one other person Tsilke would meet on a regular basis: Shleyme the distillery-clerk. He had a large family in Mistebove and a wife who was always ill and constantly on the verge of death. But she did not die, and each year she gave birth to another child. Shleyme had a lot of troubles at home. In the forest he worked hard and kept his head down.

Through him Tsilke could order whatever she needed from the city, but she had no one to spend time with, no one to talk to. Her only companion was Aunt Nikhe, so sometimes she confided in her, sharing her thoughts. Nikhe would tolerate all her whims. She prayed for God to protect the motherless child.

There were also a couple of Christian families living a little deeper in the forest: a road watchman and a forest watchman. Whole months would go by and Tsilke wouldn't see or hear another soul.

Only the river murmured and the forest sang from dawn until dusk, crying: "*Cuckoo, cuckoo! Coo, coo, caw!*"

Tsilke knew all the sounds of the forest. From the trembling of the trees she could predict when a storm was coming. And she liked—in those moments when it thundered over the forest—to take cover under the branches and listen to each thunderclap, trembling in fear, not wanting to leave. Aunt Nikhe would call out to Tsilke from the house, and Tsilke would answer with laughter.

It was as though she laughed along with the forest: Let the thunder strike—the forest will remain, the world will remain.

Iser loved his daughter, but it was only much later that she would fully understand.

When she was younger she could not fathom how a father could be so silent around his own child—his only daughter. Days would go by without him uttering a word to her. Later she grew to understand that this is how he was with everyone; even with his boss, old-man Lurie, he spoke only about business.

She made her peace with it. If her father was silent, so be it. After all, the forest was also silent: the trees, the night, the winter days—she was surrounded by a great deal of silence.

The outside world sounded to her like some faraway, inaudible echo: Grodno and the Luries, other cities and other people.

And it was only in rare moments that she spared a thought for that other world, for what happened out there beyond the woods. She left it up to the river to run ahead and greet the rest of the world. She would skip through the forest, her bright eyes soaking up its eternal greenness, its eternal youth.

The Luries were a big deal in Grodno. Legends circulated about their wealth. Their children studied abroad, only visiting Lithuania for brief spells during the summer. On rare occasions the whole family would come to the woods, accompanied by servants and relatives, and the normally tranquil forest would bustle with excitement. The two unused cabins would then be opened and the rich masters slept there. Twice a day a carriage ran into the city bringing back the best foodstuffs, wines, and sweets.

They were a privileged family, but good-natured people, not proud magnates, and they regularly gave to charity and supported the poorhouses.

When they came to the forest, Aunt Nikhe would wait on them with loyalty and commitment. Such refinement, such wealth!

She would go to Mistebove to buy food and there she would tell everyone:

"The Luries are here in the forest!"

And young people would come from Mistebove, even the respectable townsfolk, to catch a glimpse of the Luries for themselves.

The whole area was filled with talk of the rich family from Grodno who received the honor they deserved.

The forest was a place for the Luries to rest and to enjoy themselves. Everyone would play with the little Tsilke.

Back then she truly looked like a forest-elf. Her hair was curly and her eyes were not yet grey like they are now, but bright blue, the kind of blue that doesn't last into adulthood: only children and angels have such eyes.

Tsilke knew every little corner of the forest, and she would lead the Lurie children around: shoming them the river, the distillery, the road . . .

She led the way and the children would follow. The big city children were afraid of the woods, afraid to be on their own, but Tsilke was in her element.

Barefoot, with joyful eyes, she would leap about playing with the Lurie children. Those summer days were like a holiday for her. Even her father would brighten up when the Lurie family stayed in the forest. He grew more talkative and took to spending more time at home.

But Aunt Nikhe was often unhappy: Firstly, people were monopolising her Tsilke, and secondly, the Luries looked down on her like a real servant. It pained her.

But eventually Lurie's children grew older, and went off to live abroad. Only old man Lurie, a round man with a short beard and a gold watch on a chain, continued to make occasional visits to the forest. He would take Iser away for days at a time, traveling around with him through the neighboring woodlands, taking measurements and making calculations, noting everything down in his little book.

Not far away, a large patch of forest was being felled. On quiet days, when the wind did not get in the way, you could clearly hear the axes at work, and the trees groaning in their death throes . . .

Later, in the dry days of autumn, peasants' carriages would hasten off into the depths of the forest, returning at a snail's pace, laden with the long, heavy corpses of trees.

Nikhe sat by the river, washing—she was always washing the laundry—and on days like those Tsilke would run to Mistebove.

And Tsilke recalled the small boy from the old days who used to come to the forest with the whole Lurie family. He was the favourite, the most spoiled.

Sasha was his name, but his parents and all his relatives called him by various diminutives: Sashke, Sash, Sashenke. The Lurie children had a lot of toys: little wagons, toy trains, balls, and various stuffed animals: horses, bears—a whole menagerie. And Sasha himself looked like a teddy bear: He wobbled, plump and full on his little legs. He had a capricious streak but was not a mean child and he got along very well with Tsilke. Once, though, as they were playing, Tsilke refused to give him a piggy-back and he grabbed her by the hair and started pulling. It was a wild impulse and his own actions frightened him, but it was too late. Tsilke screamed loud enough for the whole forest to hear and Sasha was punished severely for it.

Afterwards they resumed their friendship until late summer, when the birds flew off to other lands and the forest grew silent and austere once again.

A year passed, another summer came to an end, and the Luries did not return to the forest. They had gone abroad. But the following year the woods were once again filled with joy.

Sasha went to school now and wore a white cap with the school crest on it. There were a pair of G's on the crest, and Sasha explained to Tsilke what they stood for: "*Grodnienskaya Gimnazya.*"

She did not understand such things. Every word about that distant city life was like an echo from a deep abyss.

Sasha, the gymnasium student, wore long trousers and a jacket with shiny buttons. He was handsome and plump and looked like the son of a general—a "*generalski sinok,*" as his father old man Lurie, the owner of the forest, called him. With each passing year old man Lurie grew fatter and fatter and wore a larger and wider golden chain around his neck.

For years Tsilke had only followed Sasha's progress from afar. There was a tutor in her house now, teaching her reading and writing and she already knew Pushkin's tale about the golden fish by heart.

The teacher was a young man of about twenty-five, still a student himself. He would sit for days on end pouring over books, studying, and once a year he would head off to Grodno to sit exams. He was always talking about how he would go to Petersburg one day to study in the university.

The teacher soon left them, but not for Petersburg—he fell in love with a girl from Mistebove who had a dowry, on top of which her father offered room and board. And so Tsilke was left without a teacher, in the middle of summer; alone in the big forest with Aunt Nikhe, alone with the sound of the trees and the secret language of the river.

Her father had become increasingly distant.

Sometimes Tsilke would be overcome by a sense of unease and a terrible loneliness and so she would escape to Mistebove to spend time with acquaintances and distant relatives there, crossing the mile and a half of forest on foot.

But she was shy and easily unsettled. The transition from the quiet forest to a bustling village like Mistebove, with its hundred and fifty inhabitants, was daunting and bewildering.

Each person had a different face. Each person spoke differently and looked different, while she was only used to seeing her father, Aunt Nikhe, her tutor and a handful of others. She felt a bond with the golden-brass colored pine trees.

She trembled like a squirrel whenever she saw a new person; when she heard a new voice she would strain her eyes and ears; new clothes, new contraptions that she had never seen at home in the woods—everything surprised Tsilke.

Often, when she was in a good mood, she would marvel aloud at each new discovery, and people made fun of her for it:

"*Kozke,* wild little goat!"

"Forest creature!" they used to call her. She would become embarrassed and run back into the woods to Aunt Nikhe.

By then she was a girl of fourteen, tall and light on her feet.

One evening, on her way home from Mistebove, her father came out to meet her, his eyes somehow beaming, only for him to suddenly break down in tears.

"What's wrong?" Tsilke asked, frightened.

Her father, a large Jew with a dark beard, always so silent, had suddenly begun to weep like Aunt Nikhe.

"What's the matter?"

"You looked exactly like your mother just now," was all he could say, as he tenderly stroked her hair.

Tsilke did not sleep that night; she couldn't stop thinking about her dead mother and about all the people who had ever died.

Why do people die? And what happens to the dead?

In Mistebove there was a cemetery with many gravestones; she had seen it from a distance. What are the dead up to in there that people need to place such heavy stones on their graves?

And in that same cemetery in Mistebove lay her mother, whom she never knew.

Dead and no longer of this world. No longer in the forest! Tsilke felt terribly sorry for her mother and for all the departed.

She recalled Aunt Nikhe saying that one day the dead would come back to life. She decided to ask her aunt some questions.

She just needed to treat her aunt to one little smile for her to explain everything. But the next morning Aunt Nikhe set off for Grodno.

She was off to have her wig repaired. Every couple of years she went into the city to have her wig fixed. It was a major event for Nikhe, one that would provide her with something to talk about for quite some time. Meanwhile, Tsilke forgot all the questions she had wanted to ask.

But she did not always feel so lonely. Weeks, months and even whole summers went by and she lived with the forest and only in the forest.

The road watchman lived there too after all, with his children. He raised geese which grazed all day long in a vacant patch near the river.

The children would play and squeal.

Tsilke played with them, although she was much older; she read them books and told them stories.

It pained Aunt Nikhe: "The child is growing up among strangers, in loneliness."

To which Iser would always reply, "We need to send her to study in Grodno. The Luries can look after her there."

His words caused Aunt Nikhe to suffer even more. She had no desire to be separated from Tsilke.

But in the end it was decided that Tsilke would be sent to live in the city once summer had come to an end.

Tsilke prepared for the journey. She was a little apprehensive.

"You'll go to the city," her father said, interrupting his silence.

"You'll become a lady. An educated lady," Aunt Nikhe added, trying to console Tsilke through her anguish.

Tsilke shrank from all those words, she hung her head, as a flower withered by the strong sun bends its head.

Eventually Tsilke was brought to Grodno and the Luries took her in.

"She'll grow up to be respectable here," they assured Iser, as he quietly lamented how lonely the forest would be without her.

It wasn't long before Tsilke grew homesick. She couldn't shake the last words Aunt Nikhe had said to her, teary-eyed, as Tsilke had set off for Grodno:

"My little dove, who are you leaving me here with? With the darkness?" Tsilke had watched Aunt Nikhe follow the carriage, constantly wiping her eyes before eventually stopping to lean against a tree and weep, surrounded by many silent trees each enveloped in silver beams of sunlight, by turns luminous and mournful, dappling the branches and the melancholy forest shadows.

Iser sat with her, wordless as always.

Tsilke turned around again, but she could no longer see her aunt—only part of their roof was visible, peeking out through the trees. Soon that too had vanished from view.

They passed new, unfamiliar landscapes, the road with its white milestones, here and there lonely trees stood in the fields and each lonely tree she passed reminded Tsilke of her silent father.

The carriage drove slowly, but downhill the horse would break into a run and in such moments Tsilke wanted to grab her father's arm and beg him to go back to the forest, to Nikhe.

She pitied her terribly. How would she ever manage without Tsilke? She had been left all alone.

They drove through several villages. Tsilke had seen many houses along the road, but now, rising on the horizon, she saw the tops of huge chimneys and church spires; the closer they got, the more rooftops she could see.

"Is that the city?" she asked her father.

"Yes," answered Iser, as if just then remembering where they were going. He raised his hand in silence and stroked Tsilke's head. Suddenly he noticed that his fingers were damp.

Tsilke was crying. Why? He understood and yet did not understand. His chest tightened and he too felt like crying.

But Tsilke soon settled herself and her tears dried up. She felt like a trapped squirrel, and an animal does not cry when you catch it in a cage; it feels angry and alone. Tsilke was a captive. Later, in the city, like a doe brought from the forest Tsilke grew apprehensive about everything, jumping at any sudden noise.

She was afraid to walk on the smooth, polished floors at the Lurie's house. She was afraid to eat from their dishes. Everything there was illuminated and shiny, every surface was accounted for: pictures, carpets, light and splendor at every step. They treated her well: the Luries were generous people, and the child had lost her mother after all. They would mention this in front of strangers: "She's practically an orphan from the woods."

"A pretty girl," someone would say.

"But still a *kozkele*," old man Lurie would add.

He was fond of making jokes.

The forest orphan, the kozkele, continued to be frightened of everything. She constantly hid, determined to stay in the shadows, while the Luries wanted the opposite: They wanted people to see how kind they were. They took her with them when they paid visits, bringing her everywhere.

On one occasion she heard a terrible whistling noise and got such a fright that she almost bolted.

"Kozkele, that's only the train whistling, the locomotive."

Tsilke had often heard about trains but she had never seen one. They were paying a visit to some friends of the Luries: likewise rich and important people, whose house was a stone's throw from the train-station. The noise was near constant. They brought Tsilke over to the window and showed her the long rows of dark red train carriages.

"And those ones, the black ones there with smoke pouring out of them, those are the locomotives," they explained.

Her eyes were wide with persistent terror; she longed to hide but could see that Sasha and the other children were calm, so she composed herself.

She was unhappy. Her father had visited twice, bringing her clothes which Nikhe had mended and washed, and each time he passed on the same message:

"If you only knew how much your aunt Nikhe misses you . . ."

Upon hearing these words Tsilke would picture the forest with its river, and the road watchman's children. She had already considered running away, sneaking out and running, running until she reached home. But she was afraid to move. Back in the forest she'd always been so fearless—she could happily set off for Mistebove in the middle of the night—but here in the city she was overcome by fear.

In the Lurie household she grew silent. Everyone said that she took after her father.

Even with Sasha—with whom she used to play so happily in the forest—she was silent.

Sasha was now a fully-fledged person in his own right, with his own important affairs to think about. He had an impressive collection of stamps and spent whole days sticking and moving them about in special albums. He would receive visits from his friends, fellow gymnasium students, with whom he horsed around doing impressions of his teachers.

He had not forgotten about Tsilke, but he no longer knew how to renew the bond they had established as children. Sometimes when the trickster was in a good mood, he would tease her. He'd picked up the word "Kozke" from his father and never stopped repeating it:

"Come on, Kozke, give us a laugh!"

"Jump for us, Kozke!"

And just as she was about to smile, opening her little mouth to respond cheerfully, a flash of indignation flared in her eyes, driving the half smile from her lips.

Everyone shared the conviction that it was only a matter of time before she would become educated. She was "wild," from the forest, but she would soon learn to be like everyone else. They gave her new dresses to wear.

The teacher who taught the Lurie children also taught her.

And yet, the more affection the Luries lavished on her, the more silent and fearful she became. In the evenings she would curl up in a corner by herself, hiding, and no matter how much they called her she refused to answer.

The Lurie's household was not a lonely place; guests, young and old, arrived almost every day. The piano played, filling the house with music.

During such visits Tsilke would sit in her corner, lips firmly shut, dwelling on unsettling thoughts.

She thought about how, back home, the currents of the stream swirled over stones, and how the forest spread its arms out over the water, blessing it. She thought about how Nikhe missed her, how her father missed her, how everything in the forest missed her, even the squirrels.

She began to hatch a plan.

One day the Luries noticed that she was missing: Where was she? They passed through every room, calling her name: "Tsilke!"

On the stairs, in the yard, in the street—Tsilke was nowhere to be found. They searched the attic, the basement; they even looked down into the well—nothing.

The police were notified.

A messenger was sent to Iser in the forest: "Tsilke has vanished!" Maybe she'd had an accident, God forbid?

The silent Iser came to Grodno and the whole city set about looking, searching.

Where was Tsilke?

In the end they found her in a village with some peasants.

While the Luries had been singing and playing in the spare room one evening, Tsilke had become very lonesome. The louder they sang, the more homesick she'd felt.

And, not knowing what she was doing, she'd left the house and set off down the street. Walking from one street to the next, until she came to a field. She walked on ever further. Fields stretched out around her, the air was filled with the chirping of crickets. One corner of the sky was still red, but with each passing moment it grew darker.

And Tsilke walked on.

A puff of breeze gave the girl a passing caress and continued on its way. The wind was happier than Tsilke: It did not need a home, and had no one to fear.

But she . . .

She walked in her beloved woodlands toward Aunt Nikhe, toward her silent father. She soon grew tired, and if it weren't for the fear that had befallen her she would have collapsed with exhaustion. She went on. Somber woods extended in every direction. But where was *her* forest? Night had fallen. Far off in the gloom—a train, shrieking like a wild animal. Tsilke shuddered and quickened her pace. Frightened and alone, she would have turned back but it was too dark to retrace her steps.

She could not see, but she heard a distant noise: the train, rushing with a deep, fearful "*hoo-hoo.*"

The cacophony subsided, giving way to a heavy silence, an immense loneliness.

Her foot slipped on a dead leaf, and her heart raced. She was startled too by her own hair falling suddenly over her face. Everything made her tremble.

Afterwards ... To this day she does not remember what happened afterwards. She awoke in a village; a peasant woman was sitting beside her, and later many peasants came, each one questioning her, but Tsilke did not respond. For the longest time her speech was taken away from her.

Who knows what would have happened to her if a Jew from Grodno had not happened to pass through the village. When he spotted her, a Jewish girl, he remembered hearing a rumor about an orphan, a forest girl, who'd run away from the Luries. He sent word to the city.

Tsilke was taken home to the forest. When she got there, she fell onto Aunt Nikhe's neck and cried herself out until her voice returned.

The peasants who worked in the forest advised Iser not to send her to the city again because it could end very badly: the child was too closely bound to the forest, such a sapling cannot be transplanted.

Gradually Tsilke became her old self again, and started to play, run and wander over the forest.

In the city she had learned to read and count a little, and so now she had a task to occupy herself: to count all the trees in the forest.

She would begin: *one, two, three, four,* but by the time she reached twenty she would already have lost count and be forced to start again. The pine trees all ran into each other like a great golden wall, and nothing came of Tsilke's game.

She was her old self again, but summer was already coming to an end.

The autumn was long and mild.

Later the weather turned cooler. Aunt Nikhe closed the doors and began lighting the stove. At night, the forest howled with a thousand voices. Tsilke was fond of those long, dark, silent nights. She liked them, and, at the same time they scared her. On nights such as those Aunt Nikhe would tell her stories from the Bible.

2

Winter in the Forest

TSILKE STAYED IN THE FOREST from then on. Her father hired a private tutor and kept a close eye on her, making sure she didn't spend too much time running around with the road watchman's children.

The road watchman, Ivan, with his large blond beard, regularly visited that large cabin next to the narrow steam in the woods, to talk with old Nikhe and Iser. When Tsilke had come back from Grodno, and everyone was trying to understand why she'd run away, Ivan shared his interpretation:

"It's the forest that called her; a little squirrel the likes of your daughter could never last in the big city. She was stricken with homesickness and it would have killed her in the end. Yes, indeed; the trees and the stream have gotten deep into her soul."

At that moment Tsilke passed by, and he asked her:

"Tsilke, do you want to come with me to the city? To see all the bright lights and the bustle . . ."

Tsilke turned pale and, agitated, she ran off into the trees.

Her father reprimanded Ivan for having mentioned the city.

Tsilke grew like a young sapling. She was studious, but forgot her lessons almost as soon as she learned them.

Nevertheless, something of the tutor's stories stayed with her. Often, wandering in the woods, she would come to a standstill, open her eyes wide, and think . . .

About the large forest.

About all people.

About death . . .

But her thoughts never found a response. The forest stood before her: a thousand mute trees gazing blindly down at Tsilke, the barefoot girl, whose shoulders had grown more shapely over the summer.

In such moments Tsilke would grow tired of her own silence, and that of the forest. She would open her mouth and begin to shout, to sing into the trees. She heard the echo of her own voice and, not wanting to be overshadowed, cried ever louder and faster. The beginning of a long, amusing forest game.

A girl, who'd grown up alone among the trees, playing with her own echo; and the echo, which lived alone on the treetops and in the empty shadows under the canopy, playing along. The game was encroached upon by the squeaking of a startled squirrel and the cries of an unfamiliar bird.

The forest lived and remained silent. Tsilke lived and sang, and—like everything that lives under the sun—sometimes she experienced sadness.

After all, the sky sometimes became gray and gloomy. A lone crow would sit and brood on a telegraph pole by the roadside, and all the trees in the forest seemed to stretch out, longer than they really were, mourning, mourning.

So why shouldn't the young Tsilke mourn too? She whose mother had died too young for her to remember, and whose father was so silent.

On days like these Tsilke ran to Mistebove, or to the farm in Prudne, to spend time in the company of others. She would return with a head full of new songs, songs which would crystallize there amid the green shadows.

During those wordless nights.

Spring and summer passed so quickly, but then came autumn when the doors would be closed and only three people would remain in the great silent forest: Iser, Nikhe and Tsilke . . .

All around, a bitter wind blew, howling, frightening, like an angry wolf. Everyone would fall silent. The adults would naturally think back to the past, to bittersweet memories. But little Tsilke, what had she to dwell on? What did the autumn breeze have to offer her? She had nothing to reminisce about. And what did she have to look forward to? Did she have something to believe in, someone to wait for?

Perhaps she should look forward to the coming summer when she would once again be able to run around barefoot and half naked, to jump into the shallow stream and kick her feet, spraying the silvery chill into the shadows of the pines.

"Aunt Nikhe, why is it not always summer? Where have all the songbirds gone? Why has the stream become so sad?"

She would bombard her aunt with questions such as these during the autumn days.

And when too much sadness and boredom had accumulated inside the warm cabin, Iser would head to the city to settle some business with the Luries while Aunt Nikhe stayed behind to darn socks.

Later on they were joined by the tutor.

Tsilke's tutor was a boy with long hair who spoke only of Petersburg and the prospect of going to university. Tsilke did not understand him, but he had no one else to confide in, and so he would pour his heart out to her.

"When I become a student . . ." he said to her once.

"What then?"

"I'll take you with me to Petersburg and make somebody out of you."

"And am I not already somebody?" Tsilke asked.

"No, you're a wild little goat!" The tutor said.

Tsilke was delighted with this answer and began to laugh and bleat and jump about like a goat.

Nikhe stood up, sock in hand, and scolded her:

"Tsilke, have you no shame, carrying on like that in front of the tutor?"

Tsilke hated to be scolded; in such moments she felt as though she had sinned terribly, and so, without a word, she would hide away in a corner. She would glance around the large warm room with the frightened, angry eyes of a captured animal.

When she'd had enough of it all she would sneak out, wrapped in Nikhe's shawl, and head to the home of Ivan, the road watchman, where there were three little Gentile children, two boys and a girl, with three heads of white hair. The walls of Ivan's house were adorned with icons and holy pictures, and there was always a smell of cabbage and other sour odors.

Tsilke would play with those three children for hours. Everyone was fond of Tsilke at the road watchman's house.

The watchman's wife cooked a large pot of potatoes, and Tsilke sat at the table alongside the children, clutching large wooden spoons, eating with healthy appetites.

Suddenly the door opened, and her father poked his head inside.

With fear in her eyes Tsilke paused, the spoonful of potato in her hand hanging motionless in the air, as though frozen in place.

Her father wordlessly took her by the hand and led her home. He did not speak, but Tsilke sensed his anger. Once again she found herself sitting in the corner, listening to the howling wind, her eyes smouldering like a pair of angry fires.

Her father remained silent.

Aunt Nikhe sat quietly darning a sock. Her lips mumbling something, she was speaking to God, with God.

The tutor sat deeply engrossed in his books; he taught himself more than he taught Tsilke.

Later, the first frost came, and the first snows began to fall. A gunshot rang out around the forest: the noblemen were on a hunt.

Sometimes huntsmen would show up at the house where they would warm themselves over a glass of tea.

They were tall, strong men and they came with dogs and guns and animal pelts.

Often, they would arrive with a bloodied, hare carcass slung over their shoulders. Tsilke's nostrils would twitch, as though she felt a sort of kinship, a camaraderie with the hunters.

Later she would discuss it with the road watchman's children.

"The hare was so fresh, such bright red blood, and the dogs couldn't stop sniffing at it. The poor hare."

Tsilke stared out the window for a long time, and wondered if the hare had had a sister, or a brother who missed it.

She herself felt the loss and clenched her young fists.

Afterward, the white winter arrived, and each day the trees took on new strange shapes on account of the powdery frost that covered them. Outlandish white forms.

Overnight, the forest had become unrecognizable to Tsilke. The trees were clad in white furs like a group of hikers: where were they headed? The world was frozen and white as far as Prudne and Mistebove, even as far off as Grodno—everywhere the world was frozen and white.

Tsilke stood there lost in thought. Suddenly a mound of snow fell noisily from a tree and Tsilke was torn from her daydreams.

She ran toward the road watchman's house.

It was warm inside. Tsilke quickly wrapped the little white-haired children in their fur coats and dragged them out into the forest. They crept around, treading over old pine-needles and white islands of snow.

The forest children had few words; they played with hands and with feet, pretending to fight, like little wolf pups.

Suddenly, several large hunting dogs appeared, dashing straight toward the children. Frightened, the children fled, wailing.

But the dogs meant no harm; they sniffed the children and ran on until they were out of sight. From the house, Ivan and his wife rushed out, along with some farmers Tsilke did not recognize. They ran toward the children and comforted them before turning their ire toward Tsilke, angry that she, an older, reckless girl, had dragged the children outside in such cold weather.

They cursed and shouted at her.

And so she left.

Alone, abandoned, wrapped in her aunt's new shawl, Tsilke felt no desire to go home, she did not want to see her tutor, or watch Nikhe darning socks. So she crept around in the forest, kicking snow dust up into the air. Sometimes she let out a cry.

And a frozen echo called back to her.

"It's not like summer," she thought, angrily wrenching a branch from a tree. If the trees would let her, she'd give them all a good thrashing. Why don't they say anything?

She wandered like this for a long time, straying quite a distance.

Suddenly a carriage approached and she saw her father—on his way back from Grodno.

"What are you doing wandering around here?" he asked, and lifted her up onto the carriage beside him.

"Nothing," she answered.

"What do you mean, 'nothing'?" Iser said angrily.

Only then did it occur to him that the child was lonely.

"Maybe now you'd like to go to Grodno? There's life in the city, other people."

Tsilke shook her head, "No."

Hearing the word "city" frightened her, and made her feel sorry for Aunt Nikhe, and for the whole forest.

What would things be like here without her? If she left, a great lingering solitude would envelope every tree, a sorrowful wind would encircle each one.

So thought Tsilke until the carriage came to a stop by the threshold of their home.

The door opened, just a crack, and a cloud of warm vapour escaped as Aunt Nikhe peered out.

The door closed again.

Silent, monotonous life resumed behind that closed door.

Smoke drifted out of the chimney lending a bluish tinge to the green and white branches of the pine trees. The other two cabins stood cold and abandoned.

Winter was settling in, making itself at home. The frost—a guest with no intention of ever leaving.

Perhaps out there beyond the woods in the open fields, the wind still blew, lifting up thin layers of snow and sprinkling it along the ditches, over the untilled plots. The wind playing with the innocent snow, unable to leave it alone, while here the forest was in deep hibernation.

Everything slumbered in such white calm: the lathered tips of the pines, the narrow, copper bellies of the trees, as silent as loaded cannons.

Colorful winter birds chased one another, singing with each swooping pass. Even amid the frost there was room for courtship on God's Earth.

A frightened hare came into sight, cocking its long ears, attentive to the sounds and non-sounds of the forest. It raised a snow-covered paw, relishing the frozen rime-ice of the woods.

Who would assail him here in such a silent world of snow and green foliage?

But in the distance the lost echo of a gunshot rang out.

The hare disappeared.

One thicket of trees had untangled its branches as though by magic; while others stretched up straight toward the sky, like silver torches. Others still resembled broken candelabras, and a little farther … look! The twisted hands of giants, vanquished by the frost.

But beneath all these images, under the rigid frost, resting watchfully, lay God's eye: the greenery, heralding to men of faith that spring would return, and that the coming season would be the best and most beautiful of all. Everyone would fall in love with such a spring. The pine needles winked and smiled.

Spring would come. It would come.

Even the frozen air carried a sudden gust, a scent redolent of summer and fragrant evenings. But in the meantime the forest remained silent. Somewhere in the distance a mound of snow fell, and the crackle echoed through the forest.

Three snow-covered cabins, and a little farther—a stable. A cloud of smoke rose from one of the chimneys and under it: a mass of crows, their blackness gleaming in the surrounding whiteness. They did not croak: they were looking for food.

A long time passed and the door did not open. Then half a day later, as shards of cold sunlight were enveloping a row of trees in a frozen embrace, the door opened. A young woman emerged wearing a fur-coat and boots with a scarf wrapped around her head

It was Tsilke.

She was off to Mistebove . . .

In Mistebove, winters were spent plucking feathers. Tsilke was a regular guest at several households. All around, people sang and plucked feathers. The plucking season lasts from just after Sukkes until Passover.

Every woman and every child was covered in feathers from morning to night. It seemed to Tsilke as though it was they who made the snow with their feathers, the snow that covered the entire forest, the river, and the road.

In Mistebove they fried goose meat and ate crackling. The frost lingered on the streets, while inside the houses it was warm, there being no shortage of firewood in the area.

So, the women and girls plucked. They went out to run errands in feathers, they paid visits in feathers.

Alongside the snow, the wind blew tufts of pure downy fluff, whiter and lighter than the snow itself.

Warm vapor poured from the houses, and the chimneys sent blue zig-zags up toward the sky.

Life was peaceful and warm in Mistebove.

Tsilke would go there to escape from the lonely forest where she spent entire days alone with Aunt Nikhe, who grumbled like an old crow only to fall into protracted silences.

Long days went by without either of them uttering a single word.

Young Tsilke resented her old aunt because she was old and grumpy.

Old Nikhe resented Tsilke because she was young and wild.

And this silence drove Tsilke to pull on a pair of large boots and wrap herself up in a fur coat and headscarf.

She fled to Mistebove.

She would sit there all day in the house of Barash the starosta, who was known for giving passports to anyone who wanted one.

Barash had a young son, Froyke, who wore shiny boots and was always singing and making jokes.

Tsilke would spend days on end there with Froyke's sister, plucking feathers and singing strange songs:

> *"What do they say?*
> *What do they say?*
> *Women like it when you pay . . ."*

She sang without understanding the words, but it was so nice to have warmth and company.

They baked potatoes and ate them with delight.

The men went to the synagogue in the evenings, leaving the women behind. They lit the fire and sang until they grew tired. The sack of feathers seemed never to get any smaller, but no one was bothered by it. At the Barash's place there was also a grandfather, or a great-grandfather, Tsilke wasn't sure which. They called him "Nikolayevsker." He had a broad, white beard and he rolled his R's when he spoke. He couldn't say more than a few words in a row without laughing.

Laughter, like clapping thunder, punctuated his every sentence.

No one understood what the old man was saying, but his company was pleasant. His old-age was comforting.

It made one think:

"Oh how long a person can live, ho ho!"

He would sit off to one side, but the feathers, those downy flecks, did not spare him either, and he would become even whiter.

"Grandad is completely white!" the children would laugh.

"He'll dream about down quilts."

"A hundred years ago, he wasn't so old."

"Not everyone lives to be as old as him," one of the old women would say, bringing the joking to an end.

Tsilke often spent the night there while the girls, Froyke's sisters, would tell strange stories: stories of love, romance and jealousy.

Tsilke understood very little of what they said, but did not like to ask questions. She preferred to grasp everything with her own reason; she had to get there by herself.

Barash had a horse and sled. One time Froyke prepared the sled and they set off over the snow, shouting aloud like the little Gentile children from the village.

Somehow Froyke managed to pack the sled with girls, while he, the lone male—young and joyful—would hold the reins and drive the horse.

Tsilke noticed something strange: Froyke would often neglect the reins, turning his attention to one of the girls nestled up next to him in the sled, and start to kiss her. The other girls acted as if nothing was amis. Tsilke turned away, angry at Froyke and the girl he was kissing, while at the same time her blood boiled with an incomprehensible agitation.

She wanted to go home and so she asked Froyke to turn around and bring her back to the forest.

Froyke obeyed. He brought her home.

As she crawled out of the sled her legs felt unwieldy and a desultory anger rose inside her.

The sled was already on its way back to Mistebove and she heard the echo of its clamor lingering long after it was gone.

Hahaha! The forest laughed along.

She stood there, staring at the three snow-topped cabins, only one of which was insulated and warm.

She stood and listened to the silence of the forest.

Slowly, she emerged from her reverie, and remembered Mistebove, the feathers, and the girls that Froyke kissed; it all seemed so far off, so distant.

Suddenly Aunt Nikhe was standing in front of her.

"Why don't you go inside. I heard that you'd come back. Go on in."

It took Tsilke a moment to understand what Nikhe had said, and she strode inside.

It felt as though she really were alienated from people, from everyone and the whole world.

Once indoors, Tsilke's aunt had plenty to reproach her.

"Why did you have to drag so many feathers home with you? Everything you touch is covered in feathers."

"Don't be angry," Tsilke pleaded.

And remembering that the child was a poor orphan, Nikhe suddenly felt kindhearted pity for her.

"Whatever my Tsilke wants."

But Tsilke did not ask for anything. She went to bed in silence and the house became quiet and lonely.

She dreamed of Mistebove, and Froyke kissing girls; she dreamed of many small white geese flying—the higher they flew the more downy feathers they scattered over the earth, over the trees and all the houses.

When would the long, endless whiteness of the world come to an end?

She opened her eyes at dawn. It was dark inside and her aunt Nikhe was already reciting psalms, the melody of her voice feeding into the sorrowful atmosphere.

Tsilke impulsively dove back under her quilt and was asleep again in the blink of an eye.

When she awoke for the second time, it was already bright and the forest outside stood by like a frozen orchestra, waiting for the conductor to give the signal with his baton.

In the meantime the frost breathed without breath and each snowflake pressed itself more snugly against its neighbor, gazing with its microscopic diamond eye at the other snowflakes . . .

And at the uncovered green pine needles.

For now there was not a sound, not a rustle.

The half covered pine branches resembled enormous eagle wings. So many eagle wings piled one on top of the other, and sticking out from underneath all those wings—little silver talons.

A flock of crows flew by, low to the ground, their wings emitting a faint song, like delicate strings strumming transparent notes.

The silence remained mute for its own sake, the whiteness was white for no one but itself.

The three houses were decked in snow, but one of them had a little path leading to it, and a few dark spots on the frozen window panes.

It was warm inside.

The surrounding forest sensed the presence of a warm house, which seemed to draw the frozen branches towards the heat. The snow did not feel secure here: every warm breath posed a threat to its luster.

Tsilke lay in bed all day under the soft quilt while her aunt danced around her like a kind-hearted mother.

A pot boiled on the stove and some chickens and a rooster strutted around the room, having been brought inside so as not to freeze.

"Such a frosty day," said Aunt Nikhe. "Your poor father; he's freezing somewhere out there in the woods."

Tsilke grew pensive.

Her father . . .

For as long as she could remember he had never talked to her the way Aunt Nikhe did, or the way anyone talked to her.

He always approached her mutely, caressing her in silence, uttering only a few silent words.

He was as quiet as the frost.

Tsilke trained her ears toward the trees, hoping to catch a sound, a rustle . . . But no—only the crackling of the firewood.

She lay in bed, gazing into the flames of the stove.

Suddenly she heard a faint noise from outside. Sleds passing, lumber being transported out of the forest. The sleds sliced through the frozen snow with the sound of blades clashing against one another.

And then all was quiet again . . . The sleds came to a halt. Several farmers with frosted moustaches had come to pay Iser a visit.

To warm themselves up.

To have a smoke.

They talked about the frost and clapped their hands together, stamped their feet.

"Some people have been found frozen to death," said one.

"There've never been frosts like this!"

Tsilke lay under her quilt and observed the farmers.

The farmers saw her and smiled.

"That's the life, eh? Lying there like an empress, all snug under her covers."

"Old Nikhe, why don't you roast up a nice pigeon for that empress of yours?"

"It's a groom she needs."

Tsilke was embarrassed and hid herself completely under the quilt where she had no idea what the farmers were talking about, or whether they had left or not.

She thought about the words: "It's a groom she needs."

And she remembered that when she was plucking feathers in Mistebove, all the girls talked about fiancés and kissing . . .

Tsilke's head emerged suddenly out from under the covers. The farmers had gone. Her aunt was sitting in the corner, mending socks.

Tsilke let out a laugh, and began shouting:

"Aunt Nikhe, when are you going to bring me a groom? I want a fiancé, all the other girls have fiancés."

Aunt Nikhe came closer, still holding the sock, and said kindly:

"It will happen, God willing, There'll be a fiancé for you yet, my child. A Jewish daughter will not be left wanting; you'll have a husband, you'll have children."

Tsilke laughed aloud: she was practically a child herself, and she would have children of her own? Some stranger would come along and become her husband?

No, she didn't want that.

She didn't want a stranger for a husband.

Aunt Nikhe regarded her with curiosity. How quickly Tsilke was growing up—already a young woman.

How long ago was it that she played with the road watchman's children—grown themselves now; one of the sons has already gone to serve in the army.

And how long ago was it that Tsilke ran away from Grodno and got lost, causing such a fuss throughout the whole province.

The old woman remembered that Sasha, old Lurie's eldest son, had visited the previous summer, and that he had spent hours on end with Tsilke.

In the thick tangle of the woods.

A boy with a girl together in the forest.

She remembered and looked at Tsilke. The latter slid a bare leg out from under the quilt and began petulantly striking the covers.

"I don't want a groom, I don't. I want to marry Sasha. He's very good to me. During the summer he said that if I want, he'll marry me."

"That's how it is, is it?" Said Nikhe, shaking her head.

"Yes, yes, Aunt Nikhe."

"My dear child! In winter one forgets the promises made in summer. Words are like the birds: they fly away."

"No, no, no," Tsilke kicked her leg and resumed punching the quilt. "It has to be Sasha; he tells such lovely stories about foreign lands. He's so kind . . ."

And she sprang from the bed, ran toward the cupboard and took out a packet of letters which she brought back with her to the bed.

"Listen to what he wrote."

Aunt Nikhe lent her full attention.

Tsilke read:

"Tsilke, it's so boring now in Grodno, but I work all day. It occurred to me to write something, a short story about you in the forest. You cheered me up so much last summer that I don't know if I will ever be able to forget you. Thank you again for the kiss you gave me by the twin pines—"

"What! You kissed him?"

"Yes, and he kissed me back . . . There's no need to be so shocked, all boys and girls kiss."

"How do you know that?"

"I've seen it in Mistebove."

And as if to tease her aunt, Tsilke once again hid under the covers. To dream and to think.

All alone in the forest, in the frosty woods where it seemed as though the trees would never thaw.

The forest consumed days, white-calm days.

Often, when the forest was especially still, Tsilke liked to imagine she could hear the whole wide world in that stillness, and in those moments the world seemed even larger to Tsilke, a whole lot larger.

She often felt curious. She wondered how people lived out there in the big cities, but she did not yearn to be elsewhere.

Yet, the kind of events easily forgotten by others were for Tsilke things to remember for a long time.

Tsilke was also greatly influenced by the story books she read. She lived with her fantasies, not sharing them with anyone. After all, Aunt Nikhe had her own world too; she spoke only of Rachel and Leah, about the pious forefathers.

Once, on a mild winter's day, as the snow was falling from the trees in clumps, scattering like salt-groats, as the inner warmth of the room melted the outer frost on the window panes, Tsilke looked out into the surrounding whiteness and spotted the road watchman walking past.

He was on his way from Mistebove and out of boredom Tsilke ran out to him to ask what news there was from the town, from the Barashes.

"In Mistebove . . ." He answered, "There's quite a commotion today in Mistebove."

"What's happening?" Tsilke asked.

"The whole town is at the graveyard, there's shouting and cursing—some thieves have plundered one of the graves."

"What?" Tsilke asked, her curiosity piqued.

But the watchman did not stop and Tsilke observed him walk until she saw only the back of his head.

He said no more; he still thought of Tsilke as a small child, with whom adults did not talk too much.

She was lost in thought for a moment . . .

Mistebove . . . graveyard . . . thieves . . .

What happened there?

She gazed through the trees. The stream was frozen. The sky peering out from behind the pines was still grey, yet it somehow felt as though winter were coming to an end. Even the crows cawed with more energy.

Spring was on the way, Tsilke thought, with summer close behind, and it would soon be time to run around barefoot again.

She considered for a moment and leapt from the spot.

She ran into the house and dug out her father's boots from under the bed: the snow would soon thaw and she could find herself caught in a marsh.

Her impatience did not escape the attention of Aunt Nikhe.

"Tsilke, where are you off to in such a hurry?"

"To Mistebove," Tsilke answered hastily.

"And what has you in such a hurry to get to Mistebove?"

"Hmm? It's nothing, just that Ivan says there's a commotion going on . . . at the graveyard . . . thieves . . ."

Aunt Nikhe heard no more than that. Tsilke had already dressed, wrapped her head in a scarf, and was gone.

Nikhe ran to the door and called out after her, but only the old, familiar pine trees heard her cry:

"Tsilke! Tsilke!"

The pines did not listen: today was the day to start shedding their snow, it was time to shake the winter off.

The snow would soon lie on the earth and, unnoticed, begin to make its way in melted currents towards the stream, and from the stream . . .

Who knows where the long winter's snow ends up. The winter will vanish with the wind.

The green earth, the dark earth, will emerge and the old pine trees will soon acquire new fresh needles.

Like scraps of life detaching themselves from the pines, red squirrels will return. The whole world, along with the forests, awaited that happy day. The winter had trampled the summer beneath its giant feet of ice, but soon enough the summer would free itself again. The sky already knew this secret and so it smiled. The breeze also knew, and so it ran from tree to tree, breathing over the deposited snow, warming it and melting it.

The animals stirred in the barn; it was getting warmer and they were eager to come out. The farmers hurried to lug their timber while the path was still frozen solid. Soon there would be no more time.

Before long the path would be covered in mud and they would be obliged to return to work in the fields.

When Tsilke arrived in Mistebove she found the village deserted. Every single soul was at the graveyard.

Tsilke made her way to the cemetery. It was a small graveyard that stood on a hill. The ancient trees, which provided so much shade in the summer, stood bare and alone, like bodies left without a tomb.

Children, old people, and parents clambered around between the snow-topped gravestones.

The shouting had stopped; the incident was being discussed.

Tsilke found her friends, Barash's daughters, and from them she learned what had happened:

An old widow had lived in the village. She had three sons, strong, broad-shouldered young men whom everyone in the area was terrified of. All three of them were thieves. No sooner would they finish one term in prison, then they would end up right back inside. The widow knew her children were sinners but she loved them and—reciting psalms day and night—she would beg God to forgive them.

The sons, the three thieves, loved their mother very much.

Because she prayed for them.

Because she was a good mother and she loved them, even though they brought her nothing but pain.

Because everybody pointed to her, saying: "Just look at the kind of children she raised: murderers, thugs . . ."

They loved their mother because she was a mother.

And now she was dead.

The three children had been away at the time, either in prison, or on a job.

Everyone in the area knew that gang. They kept the police busy, but they were agile.

The thieves' old mother had died. The villagers decided that the mother of such children should not be buried in the same place as decent upstanding people, and so they buried her in a spot behind the fence. There were those who pleaded her case: "What's this all about? How is she to blame? She was a good pious woman."

But it was no use. The old woman now lay beyond the fence, with the suicides and the other sinners.

Time passed.

When the three sons heard what had happened they rushed back to Mistebove to settle the score with the townsfolk.

Fear descended upon the town. The townsfolk attempted to buy off the three sons, offering them money if they would leave.

The sons went to the rabbi, and showered him with curses; they did not take any money—you don't sell out your mother for money.

All three of them said Kaddish for their mother and left the synagogue with angry glances.

They caused upset any chance they could.

People were afraid.

Three such thieves—bandits.

In the synagogue after the Kaddish, they would often turn to one of the townsfolk:

Why had they treated her, their pious mother, with such dishonor?

Behind the fence . . .

Buried like a wretched creature.

But people would respond: "It's too late now: what's buried is buried."

While others would say:

"If she is deserving, God will welcome her to paradise anyway."

But this was not enough for the three loyal sons.

And so on the last night the three brothers set out to carry out an unusual mission:

They exhumed their mother's body, dug a fresh grave in the part of the cemetery where Mistebove's best and brightest were buried, and there they laid their mother to rest.

It was difficult and secretive work. The thieves moved carefully; their hearts had never beat so loudly.

What if they were disturbed?

They placed lanterns beside the grave and dug and dug . . .

The three sinners worked in silence and finished what needed to be done.

Let the world know that a mother is a sacred thing, that mothers must be respected.

Hearing this story left Tsilke feeling quite bewildered.

Thieves, at night, in the graveyard . . .

She walked around among the people, treading down the snow in her large boots, but she did not hear what people said to her.

She had only one thought: her mother, too, lay buried in this very graveyard—under which headstone, she did not know; they were all covered in snow.

She heard another few phrases:

The thieves had also threatened that if anyone touched their mother they would burn the whole village to the ground.

"Those thieves did well for themselves. Eh, Tsilke?"

It was Froyke Barash, shouting straight into her ear.

He burst out laughing.

Froyke was always laughing, and he always looked at her with such eager eyes.

She tried to get away from him but he followed her, making fun of how she was dressed, deriding her boots.

"If you were a boy, Tsilke, instead of a girl. You'd be just the man to have a good drink of schnapps with."

She ran away from him, angry and afraid.

Back at home Tsilke had a lot to say about the whole event to her aunt Nikhe.

Nikhe believed that the thieves were wrong to dig up the grave, as that which the earth swallows, may not be taken back by force.

Tsilke defended the thieves

"I'd have done the same thing," she said, but her aunt did not respond.

Days followed, long and tedious, wet and foggy. Spring was slowly approaching.

The forest floor was damp from the thawing snow and the fog. The stream grew ever wider and deeper, until one morning it seemed as though the whole world would be submerged: Such a squirt, such a narrow stream stretching out so long and wide. A section of the forest was flooded and the pine trees stood up to their knees in water, reflecting in its turbid shine. A patch of blue sky rested on high, shrouded from time to time in white clouds. The water soon reached as far as Iser's house.

Tsilke stood on the stoop in front of the house, watching the currents moving, here slowly, there quickly. On the surface of the water she could see last year's leaves, pine needles, and strange clumps of dried grass.

The air around was damp and crisp. The whole forest was refreshed.

Tsilke cried out, perhaps for the tenth time already:

"Aunt Nikhe, come outside! Come and look at the water!"

Her aunt came out for a moment and reproached her good-naturedly:

"What? You think I've never seen water before?" She went back inside, returning to her work.

You couldn't tell which direction the water was coming from. It seemed as if it were streaming out of the ground, and Tsilke desperately longed for it not to stop, for the water to never diminish, for it to rise up ever higher and higher.

Until Tsilke and Aunt Nikhe would be forced to take refuge up in the attic.

Later Shloyme came by from the distillery; he was on his way to the city.

"Say hello to Sasha. Tell him to visit us in the summer; I'll be waiting for him."

Shloyme smiled:

"And is he waiting for you too?"

The question made Tsilke sad, but soon she relaxed. Summer . . . he'd have to come in the summer . . . it would all be fine in summer.

And she gazed out into the depths of the woods:

She could see several piles of snow. In that moment all she wanted to do was grab a broom and sweep away the last of the winter as quickly as possible. Quickly, quickly, drive away these boring days.

The summer would have to come for Sasha.

For all of Tsilke's unconscious hopes.

For her aunt, for her silent father who was still away taking care of the Luries' affairs.

May the summer come quickly, for the forest. For the squirrels, For Aunt Nikhe who would open the windows and take the Bible in her hand . . .

As she did every Shabbes in summertime.

Overnight the water had stopped rising and by dawn it had already begun to recede. The pine trees regained their knees, the whole forest breathed easily with a cool breeze, as the last of the snow disappeared.

Everything was waiting for something. Tsilke too.

3
Sasha Lurie

AS A CHILD, he'd been a troublemaker, an arrogant boy who always seemed to get what he wanted, whom no one would dare refuse anything. At school his teachers were less strict with him than with the others. Everyone knew about his wealthy family. He was a capable but lazy pupil, always wanting things to come to him of their own accord.

Pride was his defining trait. Learning held no interest for him, but if another pupil happened to overtake him, getting a better mark than him, he would not tolerate it.

This is how it always went:

If he started a stamp collection it had to be the very best collection. His skis, the very best. His books, in the most luxurious binding.

He was the son of a Lurie after all. He had been pampered since the day he was born.

The Luries . . .

Their name was always uttered with the utmost reverence. Theirs was a wealthy family, of good character and lineage, and they were always ready to help others.

They had a carriage with two black horses. The only Jewish-owned carriage in the city. It could arrive at the gates of the gymnasium, and Sashkele would ride home with his books like a little prince.

The whole street would watch: Look at that! He's only a boy and they send two such magnificent horses to pick him up! He rides in a carriage with rubber tyres . . . People envied and marvelled at the family's wealth.

The Luries . . .

They had business abroad; the governor himself paid them visits, and yet they were not arrogant; they comported themselves like decent Jews—to the extent possible for such a rich family.

Sasha was their great hope, they loved him very much.

And the portly school boy had the best friends; everyone was his friend.

Later, when the boy grew into a young man, he fell in love with a girl from his class. She was the most beautiful in the city. Everyone in Grodno spoke of her beauty. Everyone, even officers, stood to attention whenever she walked down Soborna Street. And perhaps it was because everyone else was talking about her that Sasha fell in love.

Her parents were poor, while he was a Lurie. And yet somehow the girl wanted nothing to do with him:

"Tubby there just isn't my type."

Sasha was plump and round though he had a gentle, charming voice and dark, shining eyes.

His enemies called him "Tubby" which greatly offended him whenever he heard it. He would lose his temper, stamp his feet, and scream.

"Tubby there just isn't my type," the schoolgirl said, and she went around with other boys and even with officers.

With everyone except Lurie's son.

It was his first taste of defeat in life.

For the nineteen-year-old it was enough to cause him deep melancholy, culminating in a large dose of arsenic which was very nearly the end of him.

For a long time after he continued to speak about taking his own life. They even found him with a revolver, though he had no bullets for it.

All these experiences left their mark on "Tubby." He grew thin and silent, broke off his studies, and fled from his friends.

Later his parents brought him abroad, taking him from Berlin to Paris, from Paris to Zurich. He stayed in Zurich for a time, where he found some peace and resumed his studies.

He made many acquaintances and friends in Zurich and in other cities in Switzerland. It was a time when the young were consumed with hatred for the Tsar. New political parties were forming all the time. The Russian immigrants, and among them thousands of young Jews, had one dream, one desire: to be free of despotism, to organize the workers. Every day there were meetings, public readings, lectures. Sasha Lurie was also mixed up in those circles, but he did not join any particular faction.

He would, from time to time, help one revolutionary or another with large sums of money.

Various factions thought that he would soon join their ranks. But no; the next morning he would head off to the mountains with a new "acquaintance." Women were fond of him and he had more money than the others. He received a generous allowance from Grodno.

Sasha studied hard and prepared to write a dissertation. He had grown into his face, which had become more refined. In the mountains, tourists mistook him for a Levantine. His appearance would stop people in their tracks as he strode by with calm, bearlike steps.

He was rarely impassioned, seldom reacted noticeably in circumstances where others would be surprised.

He was a world unto himself, one who, through his exterior calm and aloofness, drew attention to himself.

At gatherings, which he attended out of boredom, he would listen and content himself with a laconic phrase.

More than once he was heard to say things like: "There are too many people in the world, too many to share in God's bounty. We're doomed to squabble for all eternity . . . well, so be it—sometimes that can be quite interesting."

"But Sasha, one person works for the other's benefit: from each according to his ability, to each according to his needs . . ."

He would remark that he had no desire to be drawn into a discussion, and would snap with a habitual firm: "*Naplyevat*!"[1] and remove himself from the crowd.

And yet, many remarked that, if he wanted to, he could be a great orator—a doer, a man who everyone would follow. Different groups called him to them. He would smile:

"Sometimes I like the world just as it is, with all its joys and pain, and other times, when I hate it, I hate everything about it, including you and all those who want to create the world anew. So please do leave me in peace!"

No one was offended by his harsh words, but they were disappointed:

"Such a waste, a talented young man like that living without purpose."

Often, upon receiving a large sum of money from back home, he would head off to Monte Carlo, fritter it all away and return energized.

Such a feeling! To be a millionaire one minute and to lose it all a minute later.

His head was on fire, his nerves trembled: a world of experiences there in Monte Carlo, in that hell of gold.

---

1 Russian: "I couldn't give a damn!"

The others would regard his behaviour with mild contempt; when all was said and done, he remained a child of the bourgeoisie and wasn't likely to change.

Despite his minimal efforts he nevertheless finished his studies with better grades than the others. He always scorned books and those who read them and yet somehow found himself unwittingly reading most of the classics; he took an interest in botany and astronomy and whatever information found its way into his head usually stayed there. When it came to debates he was an opponent to be reckoned with.

But none of it mattered to him; not his studies, not Monte Carlo, and not his adventures with women.

"What do you live for?" people would ask him.

"A strange question," he would respond.

"Everyone has a purpose."

"And what does one get out of having a purpose?"

"Agh, you're impossible to talk to, Sasha!"

"Who's asking you to talk . . ."

And in those moments he would stretch out his stiff, well-nourished body and stare off into the distance like an irritated prince who had been disturbed by some trivial matter.

On one occasion he got involved with a woman—one thing led to another and in the end he was confronted by a Christian student who insulted him with crude words. Lurie of Grodno raised his firm hand and slapped him. A commotion broke out in the colony: a duel, there would be a duel!

Sasha was challenged to fight with swords.

He categorically declined:

"I despise such childish games. I give him a scratch, or he gives me a scratch. I have no time for such foolishness.

Many urged upon him: "We will bear the brunt of this— they will say that Jews are cowards."

Things grew heated and eventually Sasha allowed himself to be convinced.

"Fine. I will fight him, but not with swords; if a thing is worth doing, it's worth doing right . . . with revolvers!"

Both factions were shocked: it could end in death. But Sasha Lurie was resolute and he prevailed.

Rules were drawn up, the "seconds" strove to make them as lenient as possible.

And so, one bright dawn, a foreign nobleman from Bavaria and the foreign Sasha Lurie from Grodno took their places, one opposite the other, armed with revolvers.

The offended party fired first. And missed. Lurie remained calm and fired, gravely wounding his opponent. For a long time afterwards he had trouble with the Swiss police.

Sasha became a hero to many, but he considered it the most foolish thing he had ever done. The only thing that consoled him was that on that morning, as he fired his revolver, there had been an unusually beautiful sunrise, and the mountains were wonderfully illuminated.

That morning remained etched in his heart.

For a long time he could not forgive himself for having allowed others to draw him into their foolishness.

After the incident with the duel, he took a long trip through Italy. He hiked alone in the mountains and along thr coast. More than anything he enjoyed wandering among the ruins of old crumbling castles. He gazed with curiosity at the ruined buildings, not knowing why it gave him such pleasure to observe everything fall to pieces.

After his journey in Italy, he returned home.

He had left as a young lad with round shoulders, fleeing from his first defeat in life, from unrequited love, and he returned to Grodno as a young man with a diploma, which he would never attempt to make use of.

He moved back into his rich father's house and settled back in.

Having seen the mountains, and experienced the bustle of life abroad, Grodno now seemed so provincial. Everything: all the people, the buildings, even his former love—how could he have fallen in love like that, sighing for love like that, wanting to poison himself for love?

No, that had been a different Sasha.

What did he bring home with him from abroad?

Naturally he now had an education, but it was never put to use in the service of others, nor did it serve Sasha in any way.

He did nothing.

He greeted people with a skeptical affability, and paid them visits.

Not often, admittedly—the greater part of his time was spent on his father's comfortable sofa. He slept a great deal, and ate a great deal.

Sometimes he would take a book and spend a little time on it before losing himself once again to his thoughts.

Thoughts of who knows what.

A Swiss landscape, an evening, an encounter would drift past his mind's eye and . . . time for a stroll down Soborna Street.

Such boring days and such a tedious street: the Soborna, with its gymnasium pupils, who now looked at him with respect—no small thing, an educated man, who'd spent so many years abroad!

He seldom found people to spend time with, to speak with, or while away the hours rowing on the peaceful river Neman.

He was often to be seen sitting alone on a park bench, always in new clothes, but always in the same shabby gray hat, which he had brought back from abroad.

People understood it all:

Lurie's first-born had gone abroad to study: Who else should study abroad, if not the son of such a rich man? Lurie's son had come back from abroad, all educated, and was doing nothing . . . what of it? Only the wealthy can allow themselves such luxuries.

Lurie's son played cards in the club with the officers, and sometimes got drunk with them. People had no problem understanding any of this.

But the one thing they could not understand was why someone like Sasha Lurie wore such a shabby old hat. And Sasha wore it to spite them all. Always and everywhere—the same gray hat.

Girls recognized him from afar thanks to his gray hat . . .

Mostly he walked alone through Grodno's narrow streets. People haggled in the modest shops, mothers were preoccupied with finding matches for their daughters, while the provincial girls conducted love affairs.

Sometimes there was a funeral . . .

Sometimes a wedding . . .

Sometimes a fire, a bankruptcy!

How does such a city live?

But Lurie's son, the plump youth with his eternal hat, with his gaze that seemed to notice nothing and no one, lent the gray life of the city a new color.

And whenever some young lady or other walked alongside him, it aroused great surprise and curiosity:

"Haha, look who's walking with Gray-Hat!"

"There she goes, cozying up to his father's millions."

People would look with jealousy at such girls, but Sasha had no intention of finding a wife, and paid little attention to the city and its preoccupations.

It seemed as though he had fallen into a slump and could not get out again, as if he were in exile.

He received various German and French newspapers from abroad. Once a month he would plunge into them, leafing through the pages, before casting them aside.

He was often bored, and the boredom poisoned his will, robbing him of the energy to leave—so be it.

Boredom led him to strange whims.

Sasha Lurie fell enamoured of dogs.

Pugs, St. Bernards, hunting dogs, it was an all-consuming passion for him. He began buying dogs, seeking out hunters to find the best breeds. When he grew bored of one creature he moved on to the next.

"That idler is hanging around with mutts!" the neighbors laughed.

His parents indulged him; he was, after all, still their little Sashele who deserved whatever his heart desired.

In those days Sasha was rarely to be seen alone; he was always accompanied by one of his four-legged companions.

When people have such wealth.

When there's nothing to worry about.

They befriend dogs. So be it! Dogs have a right to live too, and the dogs were happy to fall into the hands of someone like Sasha.

How many times did the Luries open their door to find some shabby stranger on their doorstep, asking:

"You're looking to buy a dog? Good pedigree . . ."

"Not me," old Lurie would laugh, "I'm in the lumber business. Dogs are my son's trade." And he would call out: "Sasha, come to the door; there's some merchandise here for you."

Sasha would inspect the wares, with a friendly pat.

But everything has its limit, and Sasha soon grew weary of that too. All the St. Bernards and greyhounds disappeared from view and Sasha was once again left with the gray hat . . .

Sometimes with books.

Sometimes playing cards with the officers in the club.

Sasha remained on everyone's lips:

"If he wanted to he could have found the best match."

"And business . . . his father isn't getting any younger. Strangers are managing his father's forests and sawmills."

"Such a waster."

"Such a nobody . . ."

And yet no-one harbored any ill-will towards him.

People called him "Sashke," though not everyone knew him personally and he was reluctant to make new friends.

His father and relatives would confront him:

"Throw away that old hat!"

Sasha would laugh good-heartedly and shrug.

If you asked his father about it, he would say:

"He was abroad, it cost me a fortune. And all he brought back was an old hat, that old hat of his!"

But his father loved him and gave him as much money as he desired.

Sasha went through a card playing phase. He didn't come home for days on end and they say he could play non-stop for three days straight, taking short naps in his seat and then playing on.

His family knew all about it, but no one said a word to him.

"It will pass," said old man Lurie, and he knew his son.

One fine day, Sasha put aside his cards. Why?

He felt that it was becoming the center of his life, and that was the thing he feared more than anything. As far as he was concerned, being a slave to his passions meant being in hell, and he prefered to stay in this world . . .

He was lazy and slow to work, and he had received an education that had allowed him to avoid confronting life's hardships.

He was no fool. He laughed about Grodno, that backwater, provincial city, and the whole world . . .

And that was the end of the card playing . . .

He even stopped frequenting the club.

It was summer by then. Every evening he would take a boat and travel far downstream, smoking a cigar.

Young couples would recognize his boat a mile off in the darkness.

"It's Sasha . . .."

" . . . the flame of his cigar!"

He had still not thrown away his gray hat.

A strange affectation. Perhaps the hat reminded him of his student years abroad? Perhaps. Everyone has a curiously stubborn attachment to little things.

After the cards he spent several weeks lost in books, eating and sleeping. He slept by night and he slept during the day. Perhaps he himself did not realise how zealously his sleep was safeguarded. The servants had been warned not to bang the doors, not to make any noise . . .

Even his father would speak with clients in the furthest room so as not to disturb his son.

His son, however, did nothing, and it was clear for all to see.

Decent people look out for one another.

Old Lurie urged upon him many times:

"Come with me to the forest sometime; I have such a large estate and I'm getting old—who am I amassing it all for? Help me a little."

Sasha would shrug and say nothing.

One time though, he did answer his father's request:

"Perhaps . . . we'll go."

For his father this was a joy. He believed in his son, believed that eventually he would make a man of himself, that one day he would throw away his gray hat and put all that foreign nonsense behind him.

Sasha would become a man.

It would just take a little time, and Sasha was in no particular hurry. The white sofa seemed to fit him like a glove and lying there he could imagine he was in a dacha in Lososno. Someone there caught his eye, a splendid figure, silent, a little to his taste.

He visited Lososno a few times but eventually dismissed the affair with a wave of the hand. With one short phrase he put an end to his momentary enchantment:

"Too educated."

He was the first to bring up what he'd promised his father and asked:

"So, when are we going to visit your forests?"

"We might as well go tomorrow," his father said, not wanting to waste any time in case Sasha changed his mind.

Riding together the next morning through the pastures and into the woods, they smoked cigars in silence.

They eventually arrived in the forest. Old Man Lurie checked in on Iser to go over the accounts, while Sasha waited by the stream which was surrounded by tall pine trees.

The forest sang and a yearning took hold of the boy's soul.

He smiled.

"My father has forests and he cuts them down. What a beautiful life you could lead in a place like this, how peacefully you could sleep here."

This is what he was thinking when a barefoot girl arrived—it was Tsilke.

Sasha recognised her from his childhood.

He approached her.

"I remember you as a little girl, I see you've grown up!"

"The forest grows too, so long as your father doesn't have it chopped down . . ."

The whole forest somehow felt like home. He suddenly felt the urge to speak simple good-natured words . . .

Deep in his heart, unbeknownst to Sasha, something rejoiced inside him.

He could not find his words.

Tsilke returned to the stream and gazed silently into the green brightness of the water.

She was slimly built, and even in her simple summer dress there was something extraordinary about her.

Their silence lasted a long time. The forest meanwhile continued to sing.

"You visited us once in Grodno, didn't you?" Sasha asked.

"And then ran away," Tsilke answered hastily.

"Why?"

"I truly loved the woods back then . . ."

"And now?" Sasha pressed her.

"Now, I'm older. I long to be near people. I'd like to see what the world is like."

"The world is very large, and, at the same time, very small . . ." Sasha began.

"If that's how you're going to talk to me, don't expect me to understand—I'm a simple girl."

Just then Nikhe came running.

"Tsilke, we need to prepare some food for the guests, come and help me."

The women disappeared into the house and Sasha was left alone by the water which, without a will of its own, continued to bubble and swirl.

He lit a cigar and tried to think, to peacefully reflect, as was his habit.

But he could not concentrate. His gaze was constantly drawn towards the large, one-story house which stood so close. Simple windows with unpainted shutters. The cracks in the walls were stuffed with greenish black moss.

And from inside, he could hear snippets of song:

> "*Reyzke sees through the window*
> *That Ester's sad and listless,*
> *'What's the matter Esterke?'*
> *My lover has a mistress.*"

He had already observed her closely, appraising her. Those blue eyes, the mountain of fair hair on her head, and her bare feet . . . That's how one grows up in the forest!

He did not want to eat and so he went off deeper into the woods.

He walked and bashed the trees with a stick as if to announce: "Here I am."

Suddenly a thought came to him:

"Imagine if someone like her showed up in Nice or Monte Carlo! Such a fresh beauty, you can see the Jewish look in her eyes, if she hadn't been a Jew she might have gone completely wild in that forest."

He became angry with himself.

"Why am I thinking so much? Childish games."

When it was time to leave with his father he glanced around but Tsilke wasn't there. The sun was setting, casting ruddy brass reflections, which followed them as though someone were tracing their path with a torch.

When Sasha got back to Grodno he told several people:

"There's a steward out there in my father's woods, a silent Jew with a large beard that covers his mouth. And he has a daughter . . ."

He began frequenting his father's woods, next to the village of Mistebove.

He would go by carriage and the journey of several dozen leagues would fly by.

Sometimes he would accompany his father. Old man Lurie was delighted that Sasha wanted to come with him.

Admittedly his son didn't actually do any work there. He would sit by the stream with Tsilke, or wander around in the endless labyrinth of trees.

But let people think that his heir in the eternal gray hat is taking an interest in something and is not a sworn good-for-nothing.

On one of their trips, Sasha turned to his father and began:

"You know, father; in Paris, or some other big city, a girl like Tsilke would be quite something."

"How do you mean?" his father asked.

"Father, she's a rare specimen; she's a person of nature, cat-like."

Old Lurie, plump, good-natured magnate, had been contemplating a plan the Germans from Königsberg had suggested to him: building a sawmill and delivering finished lumber to Germany.

It took him a few seconds to understand what his son had told him.

"Hhm, Tsilke? Yes, a fine girl, always has been, but a little wild. Do you remember, when she was a child, the time she ran away from Grodno and went back to the forest on foot? A wild one she is . . ."

But Sasha, immediately regretting having broached the subject, fell silent and stared off into the fields and the woodlands . . .

Until the carriage brought them to Iser the forest steward.

From behind the trees he could hear singing; Tsilke was singing, and it was a long time before Sasha found her hiding place.

"You're here again?"

What a question. Sasha was offended.

"If you'd prefer, I can go right back, the carriage is waiting."

"Go on then, off you go!"

He strode off, and she broke into laughter.

"Fool!"

She spoke to *him*, a grown man, in a tone like that? She who never left the forest. Barefoot and uncultivated.

And yet it was so refreshingly pleasant to hear such tender words from her, such sylvan laughter.

He was not going home. They both had a lot of work to do: Aunt Nikhe had done laundry, and Tsilke and Sasha had to hang the clean laundry out on the line to dry.

The forest sang and they talked.

"She's always washing, that aunt of yours, always down by the stream with laundry."

"That's what she's like, always washing or scrubbing."

Meanwhile Aunt Nikhe felt uneasy. She has always known, it was a law of nature for her, that a boy and a girl should never be left alone together.

And there was only one set of eyes on hand to watch them. Aunt Nikhe would have to observe them closely to prevent an unfortunate incident.

She followed them, she called them indoors. But it was no use.

All couples have one thing in common: they want nothing more than to be alone together, and Nikhe had heard stories about Sasha, that he was a pleasure seeker who played cards and got drunk with officers.

Terrible.

What can you expect from the likes of him?

She tried to have a word with Iser about it:

"You're a father, with an only child, take care."

At which point Iser lost his temper and cursed Aunt Nikhe with insults like never before.

Then he left.

She only heard him muttering something.

"With my child . . . God forbid!"

Nikhe took to reciting the psalms more often. Meanwhile the forest stirred. The wind played its mute, soundless melodies with millions of fresh green pine needles.

All around, woodlands as far as the eye could see, the entire area sheathed in copper pines with green caps.

Elsewhere, high, proud trees were being chopped down, but these golden forests had not lost their joy.

The squirrels squeaked to one another.

Underneath, by the foot of the trees, streams snaked and bustled.

Hush now, forest, hush now world, the stream said; The humans are always in some hurry, building and making, doing bad and doing good.

But we silver messengers of eternity . . . we rush, and glide, reflecting back the forest, the cities, the skies. We spiral underground and overground. We flow into seas and come out of seas, over mountains, over valleys.

And why do we rush, why do we carve through stone and rock? . . .

God sent us.

We waters, great and small, we are the Earth's blood. We flow through its veins and bring everything to life.

Forests, forests . . .

Wandering among the green tresses of the forest floor are butterflies, and birds, colorful specks of life. They sing and flutter in the bright days . . .

Two people sit, a young man and a young woman, and they learn now how to speak.

They need to find words, so that one should understand the other.

Because they are foreign to each other, from two different worlds.

They are close, though they do not quite understand each other, they lack the language.

Perhaps the noise of the trees will teach them to speak? Perhaps the babble of the stream?

In the meantime they throw pine cones and twigs into the water, laughing at carefree nothings.

A squirrel squeaks, and far off somewhere you can hear the sound of an axe.

The second cabin had been opened up, and Sasha had more or less made himself at home inside. He would often spend the night. He brought books from home, and from time to time he would work there.

In truth the forest always drew him back. He forged out his own little paths, and got to know the road watchman. He had visited all the villages and settlements in the area, often with Tsilke, and very often alone.

Tsilke . . .

Once, as they were out walking—he, in his light-gray town suit and old hat; she, barefoot in a light, little white dress, her hair covered with a peasant's kerchief—she listened to him, laughing at everything he said. Suddenly she asked him:

"Sasha, are we having a love affair?"

He stood still for a moment, somewhat perplexed, and answered:

"I like you, Tsilke. You're a real child of nature, you're—"

"Don't talk to me about those *other things* of yours!"

"Other things" was how she referred to all those subjects she did not understand.

"No, Tsilke," Sasha said mockingly, "for now we are not yet having a love affair, perhaps we will one day."

"When? When?" She insisted "All the girls in Mistebove are having love affairs."

"The first thing you're supposed to do is fall in love."

Tsilke fixed him with her radiant eyes. She did not understand his words, but at that moment she liked him. The green of the forest cast a matte shine over his face, and his kind, dark eyes lit up and smiled. In that moment he thought this Tsilke knew nothing, absolutely nothing, but when she would eventually awaken from her forest slumber, when she would first embrace a man, it would be a fire to be reckoned with. . .

But Tsilke gazed into his eyes for several seconds; she did so because her aunt had always told her that one needed to look deep into a person's soul in order to know them.

He would stroll slowly with bearlike steps. Telling Tsilke stories, both true and invented. He strained to adapt himself to her, so that she would understand him.

What did he want from her?

What was he seeking here in the forest?

He himself did not quite know. He was already acquainted with mankind and the world. He had not grown tired of the world. He was not afraid of boredom—even a small thing like a cigar was enough to drive off any tedium. But he, who had never had to worry, who had never had to struggle for his life, still possessed a few lyrical cords in his soul and those cords sought to find echoes.

He often found such echoes in solitude, in peace, in his thoughtful seclusion.

Climbing on alpine peaks he had often taken in the breath of the new morning, or the final soundless exhalation of the day's end . . .

In those moments he would lose himself in thought. Leaning against a rock, entirely surrounded by the red light of sunset, he could clearly perceive his solitude.

He alone, no one else, had climbed up to these heights. Why? Why had he not stayed with them down below, with their bustle and day-to-day trifles?

He would begin to see himself as different, as a chosen one . . . until he burst out laughing in self derision and went back down to the others at the bottom of the hill.

And yet . . . Perhaps he *was* different? His not being able to mix with others, the running away to play cards, the constant womanizing . . . perhaps it was all because he wanted to get away from himself?

Perhaps he was a poet?

Indeed it was a vice he had dabbled in from time to time. He would often start writing, but would then remember what the life of a writer entailed. He thought of the poet types with their long hair, with sideburns and velvet jackets and, feeling ashamed of himself, he would tear up what he had written.

What were the singing cords in his soul searching for?

He had an answer to that too: they were searching for *something* because that is the only way they can sing.

Now, in the forest . . .

The tranquility embraced him on all sides. A year living in the stagnant swamp of life in Grodno had forged his whole body, but now, here in the forest, the barefoot girl with the light-colored eyes had woken him up, woken him like nature itself.

The cords sang all the louder. . .

But the smoke from his cigar kept all this from view; he controlled himself and spent ever more time in the forest.

The summer days were long. You can do a lot of thinking with so many hours on your hands, and with life so close . . .

The barefoot Tsilke was a temptation.

He studied her and followed her . . .

Already with uneasiness.

Already angry at himself for unsatisfied desires.

And she herself . . .

She looked like a ripe apple.

Like an apple, unaware of its own flavor and charm.

A fire, that kindles others, but which does not burn itself.

Why had they got it into their heads that she was wild?

Where was the wildness?

Jewish girls are not wild.

Sasha would grow angry at himself, at her . . .

But he would only leave the forest for very short spells, coming back soon thereafter.

At home they began to notice something was afoot.

The Luries discussed it between themselves:

"He rushes off to the forest, he's fond of Iser's daughter," said his father.

And his wife frowned haughtily.

"With our servant's daughter?"

Old man Lurie had a plan:

"Let's hope she turns his head, let him marry her, then with any luck he'll throw away that old gray hat and all his other foolishness."

If Sasha had heard the conversation he would have showered his parents in insults; what right had they to interfere in his affairs?

He would have thrown a tantrum.

He had to be handled with kid gloves. So they kept it to a whisper . . .

Old taciturn Iser . . .

Once, quite early, when Tsilke was still sleeping, Iser came in to Sasha's cabin and got straight to the point:

"I know you're a decent man. I know you don't believe in God, but you have a heart nonetheless, I can feel it . . ."

Sasha looked at him calmly.

"I have only one child . . ."

And he could feel the tears in the old man's voice. He'd said his piece and quickly left the room.

"Iser!" Sasha called out, and ran over to the window.

He noticed Iser wiping his eyes.

"Iser, I swear . . ."

What he swore was not clear even to himself in that moment. Iser silently walked off and Sasha looked out into the early morning forest. The strips of sunlight now lay much closer. The young pines were fragrant and, although Sasha was a little shaken by the unexpected encounter, his spirits soared and he waited impatiently for Tsilke.

The day was beginning.

A peasant had brought two cows in from the field and they stood there, waiting for something . . . two cows, brown like the pines.

Sasha liked the similarity of their colors.

"The forest leaves its trace."

Tsilke's hair is also like the pines.

Later, Aunt Nikhe returned from Mistebove. She had gone very early to run some errands. She walked past the window. Sasha said, "Good morning," and she answered coldly.

"Don't be mad at me, Aunt Nikhe."

"I'm not mad, Sasha!" and she went inside.

"I don't believe in God, but I have a heart nonetheless. That's what Iser had said . . . And if it really means so much to him, maybe I'll even believe in God too. I have a heart nonetheless."

It's good to have a heart.

To feel such a lovely morning.

And . . .

Tsilke was already standing on the porch of her father's house, squinting from the sun and stretching with the suppleness of a newly awoken cat. She did not notice Lurie's son, the one who'd been abroad, Lurie's son who was spending so much time in the forest now . . . Why did he come here, that Sasha?

He stood and watched her, marvelling at her every bend, at every glimmer of her half-uncovered limbs . . .

Now there's a woman . . . the kind of figure he had only seen in his most pleasant dreams.

Suddenly she called out:

"Aunt Nikhe, Aunt, Nikhe! The cows are waiting"—at which she ran off, disappearing into the stable.

She sang snippets of songs, stopping and starting and stopping again

While the forest sang without cease.

4
Froyke

FROYKE BARASH'S FATHER was a big shot in Mistebove; as starosta he was authorized to issue passports, and he also served as gabbai in the synagogue.

Froyke had no brothers. He was his father's only son, but he had two younger sisters, who were friendly with Tsilke from the forest.

Froyke was already past twenty, his father had pulled some strings to get him out of military service, and had hoped to arrange a marriage for his first-born. A number of potential matches had already been lined up but Froyke derided the whole affair.

Froyke was the prince of Mistebove, and had his pick of the local girls, Jewish and Christian alike.

He was a handsome, tall young man with roguish eyes and a round face, without a care in the world.

He strode through Mistebove and the surrounding hamlets in a pair of shiny boots. In summer he wore a dark embroidered shirt; and in winter, a long, fur-lined coat and a karakul hat.

The peasant women called him *Panicz*, young lord.

He was an accomplished rider, and could hold his drink.

He had his own circle of companions: the uriadnik,[2] the municipal clerk, and sometimes even the bailiff in Volkovysk himself.

Froyke's father gave him an allowance on top of which Froyke had income of his own: he called in favors to get people out of military service and for such services people were willing to pay handsomely.

He was on first-name terms with everyone and wasn't afraid of anybody. He caused his father nothing but trouble. How many times had it happened that, in the wake of some scandal, his father would offer to send him away to the Americas where he had rich relatives? But Froyke only ever had one response:

"I'm happy enough where I am." And with that he would head off with the municipal clerk and one or other of the Christian neighbors and go out drinking in Mistebove's lone tavern. He ate crabs and sausages there . . . Everyone in town knew about it, they knew and sighed mournfully.

What a dreadful misfortune it is when a Jewish boy befriends such drunkards . . .

---

2 A low-ranking district policeman in Tsarist Russia.

But he wasn't a bad lad, and what's more he was still young. Young people can change. But Froyke had a tendency to bear a grudge on account of a whim, or an insult, he would not apologise, instead he would wait, biding his time.

Until the time came.

Until he was drunk.

Until he lost his temper. Then it became clear that that nice boy would one day grow up to be a monster, a man quick to anger, capable of anything.

And that same Froyke had his eye on Tsilke from the forest.

She'd been a frequent visitor at their house for years, ever since she was a child.

Her father Iser was a good friend of Barash the Starosta, who in turn had a lot of respect for the Luries of Grodno who owned almost all the woods in the area.

Tsilke would pay them visits to pluck feathers and sing songs with Froyke's sisters and other girls from the town, gathering in the prestigious Barash homestead.

But back then they had been children: Froyke, a spoiled child, and Tsilke a frightened forest girl. Now that Froyke had kissed all the girls in Mistebove—as he liked to brag—only Tsilke refused to give in to him.

Instinctively, she was frightened whenever he tried to approach her.

He would bare his white teeth, like an animal sure to pounce at any moment.

Tsilke intrigued him. She smelled of the forest, of youth; she stirred something inside him. He would take her by the hand, but she'd tear it away again with such haste that it left him standing there as if he'd been struck over the head with a log.

Tsilke did not yet understand why Froyke scared her; so, without knowing why, she kept her distance from him.

Similar things happened to her in the woods. Sometimes farmers would pass through with long carts full of timber. They would stop beside the house to settle accounts with her father Iser, who would hand out receipts which they would later exchange for money.

Sometimes there would be among them a brazen young man who found the warden's daughter so appealing that he could not help but try to touch her.

"*Pashol!*" She would cry out, often delivering a slap at the same time.

Why did they touch her? Why did they look at her with such intoxicated eyes?

For the longest time Tsilke did not understand.

She grew older and Sasha Lurie—or the "foreigner" as they called him in Grodno and Mistebove—appeared in the forest.

In Mistebove there were already rumors that Tsilke was having a love affair with the foreigner.

And Froyke Barash heard about it too.

It bothered him; he was upset that she hadn't set foot in Mistebove all summer.

He went riding several times in the forest.

But he never encountered Lurie.

Tsilke was busy with Aunt Nikhe, washing clothes, polishing the copper utensils. Occasionally she would sit down by the stream to read books.

"Quite the young lady," Froyke thought, feeling a strong urge to tease her.

Tsilke did her best to avoid him; he frightened her. Aunt Nikhe used to call him a "hoodlum." She was particularly disappointed in him because back when Froyke was a child she thought he might grow up to be a good match for Tsilke. But in the end, he'd grown up to be a drunkard, a sausage-eater.

Froyke often came into the woods with his sisters. Tsilke would spend time with the Barash sisters, while avoiding Froyke.

He would bite his lips and contemplate revenge.

But on one occasion, he gazed deep down into his own soul and realized that *he* was afraid of *her*; he was afraid of Tsilke.

What could that mean?

He wasn't afraid of his father, he laughed at the uriadnik and drank with the bailiff . . .

But here he was afraid of this nothing, this forest girl who ran around barefoot, polishing copper pans by the river; he was afraid of her?

He felt something else too, he felt that he was drawn to the forest, that Tsilke's name awakened quite unfamiliar thoughts within him.

Shikses, girls, liquor, cards—there was no comparison; those were mundane, trivial parts of his life.

Tsilke on the other hand disturbed him; Tsilke was different.

Froyke came into the woods again, riding on a horse. There was a carriage next to Iser's house. The horse was unharnessed, calmly chewing on some fresh clover.

The doors and windows of Iser's place were open, but apart from the horse, there was no sign of any living soul. Froyke went inside. Bright, clean. A book of psalms lay on the table in a velvet bag, and on the walls hung several pictures of rabbis. In the kitchen, one whole wall was covered in hanging copper pans with yellow brass basins.

Froyke looked around but could not find anyone.

On one chair stood a shabby, gray men's hat and a whip . . .

Nothing more. All was quiet. Flies droned mournfully. The forest sang through the window, the stream murmured along with it.

Froyke went outside, and scowled in the horse's direction; at that moment he had a strong desire to give the horse a good kick.

He thought about it again and the blood rushed to his head with rage.

He leapt up . . .

And the Lurie's black horse received Froyke's boot in the belly. The horse jumped up, a clump of clover still in its mouth. A moment of doubt and the horse concluded it was not the intended target, and went back to nibbling at the fresh, juicy grass.

Froyke looked all around, into the woods, ears pricked, then he tore a branch off a tree and proceeded to pluck the pine-needles from the branch one by one, sucking the bitter sap from them before spitting them out.

Time passed.

He had already understood that Lurie's son, the "foreigner" was there. It was his hat lying there on the stool; he was the one who'd unharnessed the horse.

And of course at this very moment he was off walking with Tsilke in the woods, deep in the woods.

His soul burned. Like an animal, Froyke wanted to crawl off on all fours into the forest and follow them, watch them.

In the meantime Nikhe arrived, returning from Mistebove where she'd gone to buy meat and vegetables.

"What are you doing here, Froyke?" She asked.

"I have a soft spot for your forest," he said. "Where's Iser? Where's Tsilke? Whose horse is that?"

Nikhe answered reluctantly.

"Iser has gone to the Prudne forest. Tsilke . . . Who knows where she is; Lurie's son came over and the two of them left together."

Froyke heard her out and suddenly lunged towards Nikhe who was on her way inside with the basket of food.

"Listen to me, Nikhe . . ."

"What do you want?"

"Talk things over with Iser, I'm ready to give it all up, I'll become religious, whatever you want, as long as Tsilke will be my wife, I want to marry Tsilke . . ."

Nikhe turned her back on him suddenly and spat.

"Get out of here! Go back to Mistebove and eat sausages!"

He felt suddenly ashamed that he'd made a fool of himself in the eyes of such an old woman.

And the woods around grew suspiciously quiet. Many young, fledgeling birds, gifted their first song to that silence, but Froyke did not notice. He was angry and the horse he rode home on bore the brunt of his anger.

Back at home they no longer recognized him.

They thought he must be sick.

Froyke was quiet, Froyke was not up to his usual tricks.

Everyone was surprised.

But Tsilke did not spare Froyke a moment's thought. She lived with the forest.

Like the forest . . . Sometimes she was silent, and the grayness of her eyes gave way to a deep cobalt. Her lips closed like a flower, and her aunt could scream at her till she was blue in the face to get back to work but Tsilke would give an angry little shrug and shake her head.

"No!"

"What? You don't want to work? You're not going to lift a finger?"

"Nope."

The word stole out of her mouth, and not another syllable was heard from her.

She vanished.

Where was she spending time? In Prudne? At the road watchman's? With Sasha? With whom?

Anywhere else her disappearance would have been cause for some concern. But there in the forest where she was born, where every corner was familiar to her, they were well used to her whims.

It often happened that they would be silent together, Tsilke and the forest. She strode through the trees, and the trees held back their music. The trees stretched up higher in the silence, a squirrel paused mid squeak.

What was Tsilke thinking about, and what was the forest thinking about. It was as though the silence were a necessity, a law of nature.

Even the stream did not babble as loudly that day, licking every stone, moving onwards and caressing the banks with its velvety wetness.

Tsilke looked up at the trees: why didn't they see? Why couldn't they speak? She saw them as creatures with souls, some of them looked like fathers and mothers, others looked like growing children, branches stretched from one tree to the next, like hands greeting each other, like hands that caress . . .

She lived in the forest and with the forest. A little further along from the house the stream ran deeper.

She went for a swim.

The area was silent. Not one person. No noise. Just a young woman bathing.

A beautiful, young, untouched wild flower of the forest.

And for a long time she did not know that Sasha had seen her naked, in the water, and on the riverbank.

He watched her for a long time.

In that moment he only hoped for one thing: he pleaded to God and to the forest that she would not notice him.

Because the truth was that she was terribly shy.

An hour went by in this way.

For a long time she did not know.

Later, when Sasha told her about it, she was offended, but he managed to console her and reconcile with her.

One fine morning Tsilke sprang up out of bed, pulled on a threadbare little dress, so loose it exposed her pale round shoulders.

She started to sing, for no reason, for herself, singing without stopping.

Aunt Nikhe was still asleep, her father was still asleep but Tsilke's singing did not wake them up.

She had an idea: on the walls hung copper pans, brass basins . . . She grabbed a stick and started banging on the metal . . .

The din rang out through the house and through the whole forest.

It sounded as if a carousing regiments of soldiers were attacking, erupting in song and dance.

"Ha ha ha," she woke everyone up, opened the barn, drove out the two cows, and ran off into the forest.

The smell of warm dung poured out of the barn and mingled with the smell of the young pine branches.

Tsilke cast a glance in every direction and laughed silently, laughing only with her big bright eyes.

She was unconsciously joyous and ran back into the house.

Her aunt greeted her with reproachful words.

"You could have scared us to death with that banging of yours!"

Her father, standing by the window, was already laying tefillin.

How pale he was! His face reflected the hue of the forest and he looked matte and greenly pale.

Tsilke remembered that there were other trees in the forest, not just golden pines, but strong silent oaks, solid alders. They stood alone, as though ostracized by the other trees, as though they were lost.

And her father, praying by the window, reminded her of such lonely trees.

"Aunt Nikhe, what'll we do today?"

Every day she wanted something to happen: the arrival of guests, or a trip to Mistebove. But Nikhe answered. "What'll we do today? You don't know? We're going to peel potatoes and we'll have them with butter."

Tsilke remembered that she was indeed hungry, and so they sat down to breakfast.

Her father had finished praying. He was holding his trusty notebook, scribbling something down inside.

What did Tsilke care?

She went outside, she needed to test the forest.

If the cuckoo cried out an even number of times, that meant Sasha was not coming that day; if it was an odd number, then Sasha was coming. And so she waited . . .

Suddenly her heart stopped.

The cuckoo cried out . . .

"Once"

"Twice"

"Three times"

. . . and fell silent.

Her heart beat impatiently and she went to her aunt to find some chores to do. She walked with joy.

Sasha arrived later that afternoon.

Tsilke did not know that he was already in the forest. She sat by the stream, a book in her hand.

A red patch of golden fire lay on the nearest tree, fire and tree together reflecting on the surface of the water. The stream rushed over the stones and pebbles, hastily murmuring an incomprehensible evening prayer.

And on the other side of the stream stood Sasha, his dark round face appearing matte pale in the shadows of the trees. He hid behind the foliage, his gaze lingering on Tsilke's movements.

His eyes were serious, his lips closed tightly, and it was hard to tell if he was enchanted by Tsilke or if he sought to discern the nature of her character, to get to the bottom of her secrets.

He watched and pondered: Why had she surprised him so, this forest girl? Why had he run away from the city, where everything now bored him?

Why had he postponed his trip abroad for her?

"Tsilke!"

A shudder went through her; the book fell from her hand. She lifted her eyes, spotted Sasha and laughed. It took a moment before she caught herself and thought to cover her bare legs with her dress.

And Sasha thought.

So wild. Wild, and yet she is bashful.

She greeted him with a joyful burst of laughter.

At first the laughter reverberated strangely in the evening forest, where all the sounds had hidden themselves in little nests, when the shadows of the trees had merged into one pleasant whole.

A part of the forest was filled with her laughter.

Something came to life and started rolling from far off, a second later and her echo arrived.

From the house a cry rang out:

"What are you laughing at Tsilke? Why are you laughing like that?"

It was her aunt Nikhe who was preparing food.

"Sasha is here!" replied Tsilke happily.

And Sasha strode across the log which served as a bridge over the stream and sat down beside Tsilke.

"You see? I came."

"I wrote to you, did you get my letter?"

"No! Not yet, but I came anyway. I was drawn here, drawn here as if under a spell."

At the same time he looked around, observing the forest around him. Green reflecting upon green. Some pines had straight branches, while others had strangely twisted branches. The muted tapping of a woodpecker reached them from afar, and a drowsy clarity radiated through every branch.

Calm . . .

Tsilke picked up a branch of fresh green needles, inter-mitantly removing a needle from the branch and playful-ly throwing it into the water. The thin needles lay still for a moment on the surface of the water until the current snatched them up. But she soon grew bored and it both-ered her, too, that Sasha had been pensive for so long.

And then . . .

A shower of cold water landed in Sasha's face; Tsilke had walloped a pine branch across the surface of the stream. Sasha stopped looking through the trees into the clear distance. He felt an urge to grab the branch from her and in their struggle his lips touched against Tsilke's bare shoulder and he stayed like that for a second, fused to her until she stared at him:

"What was that?"

"A kiss."

"What for?" asked Tsilke, her eyes filled, down to their very depths, with laughter.

Sasha laughed too, a playful, youthful laughter that did not fit his temperament: Sasha who would walk at a fu-nereal pace and, regarding everything with the same ap-athetic detachment.

And just try explaining to the naive forest girl what a fellow like Sasha was laughing at: he'd kissed so many women in his life and not one of them had ever thought to ask: "What for?"

"You don't want to be kissed?" he asked.

"Yes and no," she answered, abashed.

The forest, the stream, and Sasha Lurie from Grodno all saw and understood that she did not herself know why she was ashamed by that "yes and no" of hers.

Under the canopy, the stream flowed, taking with it so many green shadows from the pines together with the beating of two hearts. The trees were so tall and the humans were so tiny next to them.

Sasha had respect for the big old forest and in its shadows he started to think about things he had not contemplated in a long time.

He, who had so long believed that the world belonged to him began to feel that he was superfluous . . . only . . .

Tsilke could take no more. She began to shake him by the shoulders, scolding him:

"Don't you be lost in thought too, you hear me? The forest is silent, my aunt is silent, my father is silent, and you want to be silent too?"

"No, I'm just thinking a little, it's so peaceful here."

"What are you thinking about? About that city of yours? Who are you thinking about? What are you thinking about?" She didn't give him a moment of peace.

And as he continued thinking, she grew angry with him and grabbed the gray hat which was lying next to them like a relic of the olden days and she cast it into the stream.

She laughed and clapped her hands.

The hat landed right-side-up on the surface of the stream. Taking in no water, it slowly slowly began to drift away.

Sasha stood up, wanting to save his "talisman," as his mother sometimes called his gray hat. Tsilke barred his path.

The hat swam and they followed along from the river bank.

Tsilke was barefoot and could easily have waded in to save the hat, but she wanted to tease Sasha, who could not bear to be separated from such an old hat.

The stream led them a little further into the forest, but the hat was taking on more and more water and had begun to sink. Tsilke then dashed into the water, barefoot, with legs exposed, and came back holding the gray hat.

She forced Sasha to put it on like that, drenched in water. His protests fell on deaf ears. She laughed as cold water dripped around his shoulders. Her task completed, she was content.

"If I let her get away with this," thought Sasha, "she'll walk all over me." And in his heart he was glad that such childish pranks amused him too and he was truly happy that he'd managed to forget about the city and everything else.

Repeatedly she turned to look at him, as though trying to learn something she did not yet know, and as her gray-blue eyes gazed into his, it felt to Sasha as though the sun were gazing into the forest, into every shadowy corner, and he felt like singing and playing . . .

Suddenly they heard footsteps and voices.

They looked up and saw a whole horde of farmers approaching with saws and hatchets. Some were barefoot, others wore sandals, they were speaking and looking at the ground.

Sasha regarded them with curiosity and Tsilke explained who they were:

"They're lumberjacks; they're cutting down a section of forest just beyond. They're on their way to work."

And in that moment Sasha wished that his father did not deal with forests and that they would not cut them down.

It's good in the forest; the forest is the only environment that produces creatures such as Tsilke. And where could he relax that was as pleasant and peaceful as here?

Tsilke continued:

"Father often tells me that our forest, too, will one day be sold and cut down. But I find it hard to believe."

"It's certainly hard to believe," Sasha answered. "What would happen to all the squirrels? And what would happen to Tsilke?"

Hearing the word "squirrel" she apruply launched herself onto a nearby tree and deftly clambered upward.

Quickly reaching quite a height she then, just as suddenly, jumped back down with a laugh.

Sasha stood there astonished. Charmed by her agility.

Her face laughed with childlike mischief. She had no wish to stand still for even a moment; she wanted to run and Sasha would have to run after her.

They chased each other, but Tsilke was faster and Sasha tired easily.

"You should be ashamed of yourself, Sasha! For shame!"

Suddenly he realized with joy that with each passing day he was forgetting himself more and more, that he was no longer "him."

He thought about how he'd been so serious, too serious, too skeptical about all the joys that life could offer, and now here he was enthralled with such an adolescent affair.

Running through the forest after a barefoot girl, chasing her, the forest warden's daughter.

Running like a headless chicken, without thinking. What was this? What was happening to him?

What was it about this place? He felt safe here, the feeling of being in the protection of a mother, or the most loyal of friends; every word that he spoke came from a soul at peace. He stretched out on the ground beneath the trees looking at the stream and the tangle of branches, looking at Tsilke. He felt good.

Suddenly Tsilke interrupted the silence.

"Aunt Nikhe laughs at me. She says that you have prettier girls than me in the city and she says that you'll never marry me."

Marry? Where did she get the idea that he'd marry her?

Then Sasha remembered that he'd once told her that, if he wanted to, he would marry her without asking anyone's permission.

Yes. He'd forgotten about that. But he did not feel like discussing such things now.

"No, Tsilke, there are no girls better than you. You, you . . . " He could not find the right words and Tsilke came to his aid by laughing again.

Now Aunt Nikhe was coming out. She regarded them with mild reproach; Sasha's visit made her nervous.

The girl had no mother, and she needed looking after. Nikhe grumbled something and headed back into the house.

"Is your aunt angry?" asked Sasha.

"She's a good person; but when you come she's different."

Night had fallen in the meantime. The dark forest had become a wall and only the stream made a sound. Now it spoke of everything that had happened throughout the day—of squirrels squeaking and jumping, of far off trees that had been cut down, and of Tsilke yearning all day . . .

"It seems to me," said Tsilke, "that I'll never find a place for myself. People scare me, while here in the forest I sometimes get so sad, so lonely. My father is so silent, and Aunt Nikhe is getting older and older. There's no-one to talk to."

Smoking one cigarette after another, Sasha listened to her in silence.

"Tsilke, what would you like more than anything else in the world?" he asked.

"I don't know. At night I don't know what I want. At night when the forest is asleep, I feel lonely. During the day I don't think about anything at all.

"I want you to always laugh, I want you to always be carefree."

Just then, Nikhe appeared to call them to dinner. Bright light poured out from the large wooden cabin. Tsilke dashed inside ahead of the others and started singing.

Sasha joined in, but Aunt Nikhe shot angry flames at them both.

That night Nikhe did not sleep a wink, because Tsilke and Sasha sat together by the stream until dawn.

What did they talk about? And what didn't they talk about, during those long hours of darkness?

Sasha did most of the talking. He now knew how to get through to Tsilke's soul in such a way that she would understand him. Sometimes he went too far, he would get carried away speaking about people, about long gone times, often denouncing the whole world. But for Tsilke he wanted to open up his soul and to do so he told her things he did not believe.

She listened and allowed him to speak about "other things." Slowly but surely she began to understand something of these "other things" and she asked him many questions, filling him with joy to the point of laughter.

One thing charmed Sasha Lurie: she, the daughter of the quiet Jew, Iser; she, the forest girl, who lived here so close to nature, with nature—she still knew nothing.

She did not know why he showered her with kisses, why the touch of her hand was so dear to him when he held it in his own, why he was so enchanted by every inch of her uncovered body.

She didn't know?

Or maybe she knew perfectly well, and it was nothing but a woman's game, a ruse, in order to trap him.

No, from all their talks, and from all that he'd observed, Sasha came to the conclusion that she was genuinely naive, naive to the point of childish innocence . . .

One thing she did feel: her blood was ripe and it ached for something that caused her to redden with shame. But it was all unconscious, so incomprehensible, and . . .

Sasha sat with her by the stream the whole night. Tsilke took a blanket out from the house and spread it on the ground. She jumped down beside Sasha, snuggling up next to him with childlike trust and said nothing. Later she interrupted the silence:

"My father hasn't been home in over a week."

She said this to herself, to the forest, to the stream, but not to Sasha who had begun to harbor strange thoughts; he had grown so introspective in the forest. The silence had a strong effect on him and more than once he found himself reevaluating all his principles. In his thoughts he battled with the world, which demanded something of him and from which he demanded even more. Suddenly he became aware that beside him, practically on top of his heart, a second heart was beating.

Tsilke slept and he who had already met and parted ways with so many women, he calmly watched over her sleep, and that moment was dear to him.

Perhaps it was the effect of the night, which, here in the forest, wore its blackest garbs.

Back at the house, Aunt Nikhe slept all alone. She tossed and turned her gray head many times in fitful unrest. Sasha Lurie had crept into the forest like a wicked wolf.

But what can one old woman do? No one, not even the night itself heeded her sighs—it was already on the move.

The obscurity behind the trees began to lighten and the stream appeared like a long illuminated path, rushing and drawing itself towards the morning.

Ivan the road watchman arrived to ask Sasha if he would be going back to the city soon, because he needed to know. He needed to harness the horse. And Sasha remembered that he had a horse and carriage, and that he did indeed need to be in the city that day.

Tsilke woke up and, hearing that Sasha was going away, she grew sad.

"Don't go, Sasha. The days are so endless when you're not here. Don't go," she implored him. This bothered Sasha. He resented the fact that, though he did indeed have business to attend to in the city, he was not indifferent to her pleading. He hesitated and, losing something of his equilibrium, felt an unconscious irritation.

But he composed himself and countered with a promise:

"I'll be back tomorrow afternoon and then I'll stay for a few days."

She accompanied him as far as the road watchman's hut. It was still quite early but the forest was bright enough and the morning sun, along with a light breeze, tugged at the last of the dew drops. The woods smelled of freshly sprouted shoots. A colorful butterfly fluttered through the trees, appearing and disappearing again.

Once, Tsilke would have chased such a butterfly, running after it into the depths of the forest. Now she stood and watched as Sasha's carriage departed along the white road. Sasha turned around, his large eyes smiling, and waved.

Tsilke went home saddened, and not saddened; happy, and not happy. The forest sang so heartily, everything was so bright. How could one be sad on such a new morning? But Sasha had gone away and she would wait for him until the next afternoon and Aunt Nikhe would spend the whole time glancing at her with silent reproach, and if her father came he too would say nothing . . . how could one be happy?

She went into the house. Nikhe had gone to Mistebove to buy food. The morning sun flooded the room, causing the copper pots to glisten. The beds had been stripped of their bedding, as though the place had been long abandoned. A few lazy flies buzzed . . . Tsilke felt bored and restless . . .

The world was still. The forest was still.

And in the stillness Tsilke heard the stream bubbling and calling. She remembered that she had not yet washed today and so, grabbing soap and a towel, she made her way to the water.

First she had a good look at her reflection in the water and when she'd had enough she stuck her tongue out at her own image and the gesture lifted her spirits. She kicked her legs against the current as though she wanted the stream to reverse its flow just for her, she would have liked to speak to the water, to the trees—she was alone there, alone . . .

Then she uncovered her neck and began scooping large handfuls of water and splashed it over herself like a duck again and again . . . and so when Aunt Nikhe—on her way back from Mistebove—saw her she could not help but laugh . . .

Nikhe laughed and Tsilke was glad; as long as Nikhe did not scowl at her it was going to be a good day.

The day and the night passed peacefully, with work, with singing and with sleep. Tsilke waited for Sasha to return while Aunt Nikhe was glad that Sasha had gone away.

Meanwhile Sasha was already on his way back to the forest.

He came by himself on his carriage. He'd bought several books with him, with the intention of getting some work done.

He was glad that he'd kept his word and that Tsilke would be happy to see him.

He thought about how good it was to have someone who missed him and was waiting for him. The road stretched on, level and smooth, with the forest on either side. When the horse felt like it, it ran faster; if it wanted to it slowed its pace. Sasha Lurie was not in any hurry. Neither the forest nor Tsilke were going anywhere. He thought quite calmly.

About what?

About Tsilke.

Was she one of *his* people?

He had a theory about people, dividing them up into two categories: *his* people and *not his* people.

His people were those whose souls possessed lyrical cords which resonated on a similar frequency to his own, who could always be relied upon to create new sounds, unexpected gestures, tremblings, and agitation; people not entirely laid bare, not fully-rounded, not fully-formed. Those who don't tell all and don't give everything away. They were rich, such people, rich even in poverty—people with music in their souls. When a person's soul is in tune you can play any melody on it, you can get any sound out of its cords, and there is always some music left inside them, which remains unplayed, which you did not manage to get out.

Everyone else, those who were "*not his*" people, he called "boxes," closed on all sides, four-sided, finished coffins.

Sasha steered clear such people.

Tsilke's soul was unmistakably attuned to his, its cords almost all of them untouched.

When she grows a little more acquainted with life, when she feels what passion is, it will ignite like a wildfire . . .

As Sasha was thinking this something happened to him that he would never have contemplated.

Three farmers appeared out of the forest, barefoot, wielding sticks. They rushed toward his horse, blocking his path. With all their might, they began beating Sasha with their sticks, and with their hands. It was all so unexpected Sasha did not even manage to ask why, he jumped down from his carriage and for his attackers that was better still: now they could really get at him with their sticks.

Quickly and adeptly they beat him before running back into the forest.

Sasha stood there for several minutes, bewildered. His head was bleeding, the back of his neck and his arms were in pain. He wanted to remain calm and he managed to do so, but he could not understand . . . What exactly had just happened?

Perhaps it was a dream? No, his head was in agony and he felt sick to his stomach. For the first time in his life he had received a beating. He felt deeply ashamed before the quiet woods, the sky, and his horse which had witnessed the whole scene.

But why? Why had strangers attacked him?

He did not lose his composure; he went over to the tiny stream that ran in the ditch alongside the road, washed his head and stood still for a moment.

Tsilke was still waiting for him, she was overjoyed and then shocked when she noticed the bloodstains on his clothes.

"What happened?"

Sasha laughingly told her about the ambush on the road. Aunt Nikhe came out and overheard the whole thing. She ran into the house to fetch water and clothes, and they bandaged Sasha's head.

"But who and why?"

Tsilke thought for a moment and suddenly let out a cry

"It was Froyke's doing . . . Froyke's handiwork!"

"Who is this Froyke?" Sasha urged.

And Tsilke started to tell him about Mistebove, about the long winter nights plucking feathers, about Froyke and the girls he used to kiss. The whole childish story of her's floated before Sasha's eyes as she told it.

She continued speaking, seeming to forget all about what had happened and the fact that Sasha had been injured. Sasha himself forgot what had happened to him on the road, so vivid and alive was her story, describing summer after summer, winter after winter. Days and years swam past and into those days wandered a certain Froyke with shiny boots, a fellow who kissed all the girls and got drunk with the bailiff, a Froyke whom everyone in the area was afraid of. And now it seemed that this Froyke was the one who had sent three farmers to break Sasha's bones all because Tsilke wouldn't let Froyke kiss her?

"And why didn't you let him kiss you if all the other girls let him?"

Tsilke fell silent and hung her head.

That same evening Iser returned to the forest and stayed for several days.

In the morning old man Lurie arrived accompanied by some merchants. The forest bustled with people from the city. Aunt Nikhe and Tsilke were working.

Sasha wandered by himself, reading books. The woods relaxed him, but his mind often returned to the beating he'd received.

The thought of it would not allow him to rest and he managed to talk himself into a little mission: he set off for Mistebove.

On the way he though back to the boxing moves he'd once learned from a friend in the mountains.

"You hit your opponent with your right hand, and you defend yourself with your left; you're allowed to hit anywhere except below the belt; if your opponent has glasses you can't punch him in the face . . ."

It would be a shame if this Froyke fellow wore glasses. No, a playboy like that wouldn't wear glasses. People who wear glasses are cold blooded . . .

Sasha walked and thought:

People have hands and sometimes they have to get them dirty.

Once he reached Mistebove he called on Froyke.

No glasses, he remarked.

"I am Alexander Lurie," he introduced himself, "from Grodno, Sasha Lurie. My father owns forests here. He's just now bought a new forest in Svislotsh, we need someone . . ."

Froyke glared at him askance and strode toward him.

"What do you want from me?"

"I've heard that you're without work, perhaps you'd like to fill the position . . ."

"Me, in the forest?" Froyke said, surprised.

Sasha walked with him ever further away from his house and closer toward the field, which had been his intention: to lead him out into an open space.

And once in the field . . .

Sasha wasted no time.

"A week ago, as I was riding through the forest, I was attacked and beaten by three farmers. Nobody knows me here, I haven't done anyone around here any harm, yet there is a suspicion that it was you who put them up to it . . ."

Froyke bit his lip and said nothing.

His silence deflated Sasha's anger. A silent person feels regret and that is disarming. Sasha sprang forward and grabbed him by the hand.

"You admit it, do you? You were the one who . . . "

But Froyke jerked his hand away and prepared to fight.

A moment passed . . .

And Sasha's fists began showering Froyke's face and body with punches. He was the attacker, on the offensive, though Froyke launched himself into the fray with all his force. They fought without any method, kicking, punching, biting . . .

Sasha—the bearlike, plump young man—was the winner. He lay on top of Froyke and just waited for him to surrender, and if he so much as moved, Sasha treated him to another shower of punches.

Afterward Sasha picked himself up. Froyke was left lying on the ground, covered in bruises. Their scuffle had disturbed a patch of the earth around them. Sasha spoke angrily and agitated:

"Setting three people with sticks on someone, three against one, that's the lowest of the low, and now you've paid for it . . ."

Froyke was silent. The whole thing was so unexpected and he'd suffered a good beating. He was silent, guilty and afraid, and Sasha started to leave and went off, relieved, towards the forest where he did not say a word about what had just happened.

That same evening Iser left again. Nikhe was once again deeply unsettled while Tsilke and Sasha lit a campfire in the forest and sat looking into the flames. Later the forest watchman came by and reprimanded them for lighting a fire in the woods. But when he saw that it was Lurie's son he took off his hat, sat down with them, and spoke about forests, about aristocrats, and about hunting . . .

And as he spoke, the watchman himself threw some dried twigs onto the fire.

5
Tsilke Finds Out . . .

FROYKE KEPT QUIET about the whole incident and no-one in the village learned of his defeat. Froyke himself had made peace with the fact that the young Lurie had beaten him up.

It was Lurie, after all. If Froyke had been attacked by somebody else, someone more like himself, it would have pained him considerably more, and then he would not have held his tongue.

But after that day Froyke changed. He became calmer. From time to time he might still have a few too many drinks and lose the run of himself, but he no longer chased after every *shikse* that crossed his path. He had also stopped ridiculing everyone, and began giving his father a helping hand with his business, helping him transcribe his papers and doing everything that old Barash asked of him.

He could often be seen sitting by himself outside the house. He would sit silently with a cigarette in his mouth, thinking, thinking . . .

Over there, three kilometers away, was the Lurie's forest . . . Over there . . . She was running around barefoot in a light little dress . . .

And the Lurie boy who had given Froyke a hiding, was at that very moment feasting his eyes on her bare legs, her uncovered neck. They stay alone for hours on end and no one says a word to them . . . He's Lurie's son after all, the rich man's son, the educated "foreigner."

Froyke smoked in silence, plagued by anger and pain, staring down at his boots which were no longer as polished as they had once been. Somehow he'd lost interest in everything, the whole world and all the girls in it too.

The girls of Mistebove for their part felt that their "Samson" was no longer the hero he once was; they gathered in corners to joke about him, and then said to his face:

"Froyke, you're in love . . ."

"Froyke, Tsilke is a nice girl, but she prefers Grodno to Mistebove, doesn't she?"

He would respond with anger, before running off to play cards, with the municipal clerk, or the baker's son. In the summer they played in the wheat-fields just outside the village. The wheat had already been cut there, while elsewhere the work had only just begun. In the shadow of a tree, a couple of wasters lay playing cards for long hours.

Froyke almost always won, but on the way home he would become distant from his friends. His winnings, clinking in his pockets, no longer gave him pleasure.

Something nagged inside him—he yearned for Tsilke.

But Tsilke did not even want to speak to him.

There in the forest, not far from Iser's house a family of gypsies had set up camp: ten or so adults with a whole gang of young little gypsy children who ran around as naked as animals . . .

They settled in the forest under the trees. Large canvas tarpaulins lay on the ground, and there were two carriages with untethered horses, several dogs lying quietly nearby, along with piles of brass cauldrons, pitchers, buckets and strange, tattered garments of old velvet.

One gypsy sat nursing a baby. She uncovered her breast entirely and in the shadows of the forest her body seemed even darker.

Tsilke could not help but stare at the mother gypsy the most; Tsilke felt an overpowering curiosity toward her. Meanwhile the little baby kept its eyes closed, and suckled.

The older gypsies wandered around the area, exploring the nearby villages. The little naked ones tore around through the forest, dancing in the stream, and it seemed as though at any moment they would start clambering like the squirrels in the trees.

Tsilke was overjoyed that the gypsies had come to the lonely forest; Sasha had been in Grodno for several days already.

Why had he gone away?

She did not know, she did not understand him.

One minute he would come to her, and say the kindest words to her, telling her many things—not all of which she understood—and the next minute he'd fall silent, like a stranger, and run away from the forest.

Why?

Clearly he must be getting bored here, or perhaps there were other people in the city he was drawn to.

Tsilke now spent whole days with the gypsies, though her aunt angrily insisted that she shouldn't have anything to do with them: they eat tobacco and perform witch-craft—you need to watch out for them!

The locals were afraid that they would steal things. Shleyme from the distillery came to stay at Iser's house. The road watchman was also keeping an eye on them.

At night the gypsy campfire lit up the forest. They cooked food and smoked pipes around the fire.

Black-beared men with matted hair spoke in their strange, harsh language. Often they sang all together in unison. But one of them, the old man, blind in one eye— Karaho, they called him, which in gypsy language means "blind-man"—always remained silent and one had the impression he was harboring many terrible secrets.

Tsilke would come to talk to them, to study with open, curious eyes the "strange folk" as her aunt Nikhe called them.

From Mistebove and the nearby farms, girls and boys would come to see the gypsies and have their fortunes told.

Froyke also came from Mistebove, he quickly befriended the whole bank, drinking with them and playing cards. One time he accepted an invitation to dance with a young gypsy girl. She wore several thick necklaces with red beads around her neck and her speckled floral dress reached all the way down to the ground.

She had a round, dark face, and large green eyes like two unripe wild apples. Her neck seemed as black and shining as if it were smeared in pitch. Her figure was slim, her posture stiff. She threw her arms around Froyke and dragged him off to dance; shouting something to her friends who responded—between puffs of smoke—with roars of laughter.

Tsilke approached them. She felt somehow drawn to the dancing pair. In that moment she was jealous.

They danced one karahod, then another.

Froyke and the gypsy girl danced slowly, drifting away from the group, deeper and deeper into the tangle of the forest.

The other gypsies took no further interest in the two missing dancers. But Tsilke's heart began to beat faster with a bewildering curiosity.

She gazed constantly in the direction where Froyke had gone, but she could not see or hear a thing.

That had been in the evening. Meanwhile night had fallen and there was still no sign of Froyke and the gypsy girl.

Tsilke was restless and agitated. She was thinking about Froyke, about the gypsy girl. All the girls loved Froyke, and they all let him kiss them—why, when Tsilke had kept him at arm's length, was she now thinking about him, pictured him now tossing his head and dancing?

She spent an unsettled night.

Several times, she approached the window and gazed outside.

She saw the road watchman come and stamp on the last sparks of the campfire, grumbling and cursing to himself.

The next morning, Froyke returned. He lingered outside Iser's house but when he met Tsilke he pretended he just happened to be passing.

"Why don't you come to Mistebove?" he asked.

Tsilke lost her temper and said:

"Go! Go to your gypsy girl!" and she went to find her aunt Nikhe.

Froyke stood for a moment, deep in thought. Then he let out a triumphant whistle.

Ha ha ha, it bothers her. That's good!

And he set off to join the band of gypsies who were wandering the forest searching for berries.

That afternoon Tsilke began to wish Sasha were there; the fact that Froyke was lurking around in the woods with the gypsies made her uneasy.

Her father came home for a few hours before heading off again. Her aunt did not leave the house—she was keeping her distance from the gypsies.

Tsilke felt a heavy tedium and she decided to visit Prudne.

It was already late-summer. New melodies had arrived in the forest, brought by the fledgeling birds. These new notes were easily distinguished from the old, yet the forest's song was constant. The birds let out bursts of song, long and short, lasting seconds and minutes, happy moments and nostalgic ones. It sounded as if one bird were calling out to someone, while another punished them with its noise . . . and there, a cricket in a dark corner, believing it was evening already, was about to carve the air with its chirping, only to stop abruptly—it was still day.

Tsilke walked to Prudne. She reached the road, glancing in both directions along the white band which seemed to stretch off into infinity, and re-entered the forest on the other side. Suddenly she saw a pair of bare feet, and next to them more feet, these ones wearing boots . . .

It was Froyke and the gypsy girl . . .

They were lying next to each other. The girl's hair was unbound and disordered, her green eyes fixed Tsilke with mocking hostility . . . Froyke let out a whistle.

His black shirt was unbuttoned revealing a portion of his hairy torso. He noticed Tsilke turn away and leave. Springing to his feet, he ran after her.

"Tsilke!" he shouted.

She stopped.

"What do you want?"

Froyke appeared to be drunk and she was ready to defend herself if needs be. They called her Tsilke the Wild after all, and she had a strong pair of arms—just let him try anything, that Froyke.

"What do you want?" she asked again, not quite sure why: she was waiting for an answer; she wanted him to say something.

Froyke wanted to explain it all in one scream . . . to let everything out, all of his sorrows, to tell her that his life was meaningless without her. She only had to say the word, and he would give up the gypsy girl, and everyone else. But instead he said:

"Lurie, that foreigner, will drive you crazy: he'll make you unhappy . . ."

Just then, the gypsy girl rose to her feet. She ran toward Froyke, grabbed him and would not let him go.

Tsilke backed away. Taking one last glance she saw the gypsy's arms wrapped around Froyke. He too stretched out his arms and fell on her with kisses . . .

Tsilke walked on. She wanted to think about Sasha . . . Yes, tomorrow, or the day after, he would come and stay for several days, he would . . .

But as she was thinking, she felt two pairs of eyes on her: the gypsy's eyes and Froyke's.

Froyke's eyes . . . "*He'll only drive you crazy, that foreigner.*" Why had he said that to her? She drove the thoughts away, but as she was nearing Prudne she once again pictured them lying together, arms entwined.

Tsilke was disconcerted, her heart beat faster . . .

She arrived in Prudne.

It was a place she visited from time to time. She had friends on the farm there—the shepherd's daughters.

Two tall, solidly-built girls with coarse faces. They looked ten years older than they really were. Always somewhat drowsy, their clothes hung on them gracelessly. They worked a great deal, but always slowly and lethargically, as though half asleep . . .

And Tsilke?

Tsilke visited the "sleepy girls,"—as they were called—in search of company. Every now and then she was overcome with a yearning to run off to someone, to hear another person's voice, another person's laugh.

Despite how bound she was to the lonesome forest, how used she was to the silence, she would sometimes run to Mistebove, or to Prudne.

She divided her visits as follows:

In winter she went to Mistebove, where they plucked feathers day and night. And in summer, she went to Prudne.

The shepherd had a large house with many windows. During the summer all the windows were open and swarms of flies laid siege to every morsel of food. Several American photographs hung on the whitewashed walls, along with two tefillin pouches. The house was always empty, doors and windows, always open. Every member of the family was working somewhere. The shepherd and his son would drive into town while the sleepy girls and their sleepy mother washed the milk cans. They were always busy, always bustling.

A little further on from the shepherd's house there stood another house with painted shutters and brown ledges over the windows. In that house lived the Arendar, the leaseholder of the whole farm, an angry Christian with a pointy moustache and beady, scornful eyes. He always walked around with two large dogs and you could hear him shouting from one corner of the yard to another.

There was also a large orchard, a gardener and other laborers.

For Tsilke, coming from the empty forest, there was a lot there to see and hear. That alone was reason enough for her to come visit.

Sometimes a spark of youthfulness would flicker within the two sleepy girls in the mischievous Tsilke's company.

They would tell her things that happened in Mistebove or in Grodno—they spoke often about the "big city".

Tsilke often followed them out to the field. In Summer— wheat-fields stretched into the distance, punctuated by dark copses of trees, which appeared like black ships on a sea of gold.

The woods looked like fences, like black palaces. Young Gentile rascals would walk by, laughing and joking, assailing the women with curses.

And once, in early summer—Tsilke remembered it well—one of the shepherd's daughters was separated from them and hid herself amid the tall wheat. Tsilke heard laughter from inside the wheat, she trembled, and kept silent, asking the second sister nothing . . . she did not understand, while at the same time she almost understood. There was still something that she didn't know.

Why did Froyke Barash try to kiss all the girls with such ardor? And why were the girls ashamed to be kissed?

And those nasty Gentile boys of the Prudne fields . . .

They stare with such curiosity at the girls' bare legs . . . why is that?

And Tsilke herself, when she heard the shepherd's daughter laughing in the wheat, her entire body trembled, and the blood began to surge inside her veins.

She strode across the sun-warmed ground, walking alongside the second sleepy girl, who bent down towards the ground, plucked a flower, unwilling to speak.

Two women sharing a silence, while a third laughed out there in the wheat-field with the young farmer . . .

Now Tsilke was back in Prudne once again

She approached the house and heard wild cries coming from inside. She looked in through the window and saw the following scene: the shepherd and his fat wife, his son, all of them together were beating the sleepy girl who had hidden that day with the young farmer in the wheat-field.

Her clothes were tattered, her body bleeding, her hair disheveled. She stood before them, large and ungainly with exhausted eyes and sluggish movements; it looked as though all she wanted to do was sleep.

But her parents and brother continued to beat her and beat her: "A bastard, she's going to bring us a bastard!

The other daughter was hiding behind the house; Tsilke went to her.

"Why are they beating your sister?"

"Why? You don't understand? She's going to have a baby."

"A baby? She's going to have a baby, and that's why they're beating her? And if I have a baby will they beat me too?"

"You're an idiot . . ." the girl said angrily.

"Explain to me then, why are they beating your sister?"

"Her child will be a bastard. Do you remember at the start of the summer, in the wheat-field , she was with that peasant boy . . . you remember how they laughed?"

Tsilke remembered all too well, but she did not quite understand what it all meant. The cries could still be heard coming from inside the house; they screamed like drunkards. The whole scene left Tsilke shocked and disconcerted.

To the forest, back to the forest.

Trees and the shadows of trees—Tsilke lost herself in the shadows. Night was falling. It was almost dark, but she knew the way back to her father's house; there wasn't a path through the trees that she didn't know like the back of her hand.

But the ways of people, their confusion and passions, were so alien to her, so unfamiliar.

She came home that day with a heart full of questions.

But who was there to speak to? Who could she ask?

Aunt Nikhe listened to the whole story and reproached Tsilke for having disappeared from the house.

But later, in the hours of evening and night, Tsilke did not leave her aunt's side, posing questions all the while. Why after why:

"Why did they beat the shepherd's daughter like that?

"And what is a 'bastard' exactly anyway?"

Aunt Nikhe shook her head sadly.

The shepherd and his children . . .

They lived so far from other Jews, in such close proximity to the farmers that they were beginning to resemble farmers themselves, becoming like animals.

"But, Aunt Nikhe, what did the shepherd's daughter do wrong?"

Nikhe hesitated and blundered, giving Tsilke a wise, good natured smile. Suddenly her smile seemed to grow younger and younger . . . an almost girlish charm spread over Aunt Nikhe's face.

"They call you a wild *Kozke*, my dear Tsilke, and it's true . . . you still know nothing."

"What don't I know?"

"What all the other girls your age know already."

"What do they know?"

It was already night, though some red still shone through the window, through the trees, a remnant of the lingering daylight hitting the copper utensils on the wall causing them to burn with cold fire.

Crickets chirped outside, the sound resembling a steady beat on tiny drums.

That night Nikhe recounted for Tsilke—slowly and tactfully—the story of her youth, and her wedding.

Piously reserved and with a pang of dread, Aunt Nikhe confided in Tsilke everything that "all girls of her age already know." Tsilke curled up next to her, eyes closed, and listened as her aunt spoke . . .

It felt as though the old forest had grown a tongue and was recounting all the secrets of life. But had she not already known it all? Indeed. It seemed she *had* known it all, but she had not understood: she had felt it but she had not comprehended.

Luckily it was dark in the house and Aunt Nikhe could not see that she was blushing the whole time.

Nikhe often let out a sigh, a sigh that meant:

"*Child, child! Years go by and years fly. Tsilkes like yourself become mothers, and those mothers become grandmothers. . . the years fly by . . .*"

Nikhe stroked Tsilke's head, her hair, which the dew had made damp and fragrant; she caressed and held the forest orphan close to her, reminding herself that she too had once been young.

Nikhe decided to light a fire. Tsilke slipped out of the house. She sat on the porch and gazed out into the woods. The gypsies were cooking something, but it did not entice her toward the campfire . . .

"So, that's how it is . . ." she said to herself several times, "I knew it all" and her body winced . . . "I didn't know it," she thought again and images came back to her from the previous days. She thought of the girls in Mistebove, who often spoke such incomprehensible words, thinking that Tsilke understood them. They had laughed, and Tsilke had laughed along with them many times, though she had not understood what they were laughing at, or why. A lot of things made sense now.

That's why the sleepy girl had hidden that time in the corn . . .

And Froyke with the gypsy girl earlier that morning!

And the way Sasha often kissed her: her face, her throat, the nape of her neck . . . Oh, let him come now and she'd kiss him too, she would kiss him over and over again.

The thought frightened her: "And what if we're not supposed to?"

She went to bed, full of sweet restlessness. In her sleep someone chased her across a cornfield. She fled, and yet strongly wished that he would catch her—it was Froyke with his boots, with his black shirt. She ran and laughed . . . ran and laughed . . .

No one saw her running, but Nikhe heard her laughing in her sleep and she rushed over to her bed:

"Tsilke, what's with you, why are you laughing?"

She woke up and began cursing Froyke.

"What has Froyke to do with anything, merciful heavens!" Nikhe spat out three times and mumbled something.

Later they went back to sleep. Shleyme from the distillery slept on the porch; he was guarding the house from the gypsies. The forest slept—the whole world slept. And if a breeze took it upon itself to give the pine branches a shake—the branches would hiss for a moment, only to return again to their slumber.

A great silence enveloped the forest, and if there was anything sighing in such a quiet night it was the silence itself . . .

Tsilke awoke before Aunt Nikhe. She looked over to her aunt's bed, at her old face and gray head, and felt a deep pity for the old woman. "She will never again kiss anyone again, she has already lived out her life."

Tsilke made her way quietly out the door, out onto the porch. Shleyme's bed was already empty, Shleyme himself had already gone to the distillery.

She began looking around for the gypsy boys who were usually up by now, running and horsing around in the forest. But there was no one there. No one . . .

She ran down from the porch and searched the nearby woods: left, right, nothing, empty. The place where the gypsy camp had been was now an empty space with black burnt patches on the earth. There were a few severed chicken heads lying around, a piece of string, a torn sleeve from some old garment . . . and nothing more.

For a moment, Tsilke felt sad—everything that went away and vanished from sight, everything that was there one day and gone the next, left behind a painful yearning in Tsilke's soul . . .

No more gypsies—a lonesome, empty forest. Just the same trails between the trees remained, the same green of the needles, the same stream . . .

The stream . . .

It always spoke the same language, it ran eternally along the same course, carrying on its hunched shoulders the shadows of the high pine trees. It did not pause for even a moment as it passed Tsilke—sitting now by its banks with her finger in her mouth, like a young girl—It did not ask her:

"Tsilke, what are you thinking about?"

No. Not a single tree, not a single bird: no one asked Tsilke what she dreamt or mourned, or why she was now ashamed to go back inside and look her aunt in the eye . . .

The night before Aunt Nikhe had confided strange things in her.

Hahaha!

And it seemed to her that it hadn't been yesterday but long ago, years ago, lost in the depths of Tsilke's memory. Now she remembered . . . now.

"Tsilke!"

It was Aunt Nikhe, it was time for work. Iser was coming home today.

They worked in silence, cleaning every corner. The beds were already made and covered in white cushions.

Spick and span. After breakfast, Nikhe took a basket and headed for Mistebove.

Before leaving she adjusted her wig without even glancing in the mirror. She caressed Tsilke's head several times before going out the door.

And once she was gone Tsilke burst into tears. Without rhyme or reason, without pain she cried, and she felt so good afterwards, when the tears stopped coming.

She was alone now in the great forest. The windows were open and the green of the needles and the gold of the pines filled the house with forest, with calm forest.

She sat down by the window and watched the chickens creeping around, one by one, looking for food. She stared at one tree and another, wondering which one had the most branches.

Suddenly she began to smile to herself and the smile spread slowly over her face, over her lips, to her eyes . . . The smile spread to every tree, through the whole forest and culminated in a short "hahaha."

Who or what was Tsilke laughing about? The forest neither knew nor inquired.

In the meantime the sun swam overhead. Sometimes a whole sea of light poured down onto the forest, and in those moments the birdsong rose higher. The sunbeams and the sounds blended together and every sound and every trill resonated with clarity. And when the sun moved aside, shadows lay down over every tree, over every trail, and a cool-warm breeze blew. Everything then became more restrained. There was no mourning in the forest, the birds did not fall silent, but there was no rejoicing either until the sun once again returned to pour light onto various parts of the woods; silver beams enveloping the trees and on the tip of every needle shone an illuminated diamond . . . Then even more noises could be heard, such sounds that only converse with the beams, only with the lofty blue which flows so peacefully for everyone, for the whole forest, and for no one . . .

Tsilke sat for a long time, lost in thought. She was surprised that Sasha had not yet returned.

Sasha. . .

What kind of a person was he? And was it true what he once said, that if she wanted, he would marry her? He had only said it once, but she remembered it well. Supposing it were true; if she wanted to, if he did indeed marry her, where would they live? Here in the forest, or in Grodno? In Grodno no doubt; Sasha would not be able to sit still in the forest. But in Grodno there would be so many unfamiliar people, all those streets and buildings—everything would be unfamiliar.

She thought about Sasha, when suddenly the image returned to her of Froyke and the gypsy girl danced away together, deeper and deeper into the woods. . .

No, the gypsies had left. The uriadnik and several farmers came to Iser's house and asked Tsilke:

"When did the gypsies leave?"

"How long were they here and what did they steal?"

In the surrounding villages and in the nearby farms they had caused quite a stir.

Nikhe returned from Mistebove, she had lingered quite a while in the village that day.

Why?

She explained to Tsilke that the Barashes had invited her to their house and had spoken to her for a long time. They'd spoken about Tsilke in fact. It was time for her to start thinking about marriage, and they had a son of marriageable age . . .

Admittedly he was still a bit wild, that son of theirs, but he'd make a man of himself soon enough, he'd said so himself. He had already spoken to Nikhe several times. When Nikhe brought it up with Iser he grew angry: "No daughter of mine," he shouted, "is ever going to marry that sausage-eater!"

Tsilke stood in the middle of the room, stretching herself as though waking from a slumber, and said to Aunt Nikhe:

"That's enough about weddings, and about Froyke: wasn't he just the other day dancing with a gypsy girl?"

"Where did he dance? When was this?"

Tsilke told her about everything she had seen in the forest, about Froyke and the gypsy.

Just then they heard the sound of an approaching horse.

Nikhe announced:

"That'll be your father now. . ."

But Tsilke recognized the trot of Lurie's horse.

"No, it's Sasha."

In a flash she was outside, her laughter ringing out for all the forest to hear.

"How happy she is to see him," Nikhe thought, "It will all lead to disaster, disaster I tell you . . ."

Sasha had brought sweets, chocolates and books. They left the gifts lying on the ground and went off to find the road watchman, Ivan, to let him take care of the horse.

They walked and laughed and talked. Tsilke told Sasha all about the gypsy girl and the sleepy shepherd girls of Prudne, but she said nothing about the conversation she'd had with her aunt, and nothing about her dreams that night. Suddenly she could no longer hold it in and she laughed again happily, to herself this time—and to no one else.

"What's so funny? Sasha asked.

"I was just remembering something."

"What?"

"That girls become mothers and mothers become grannies."

"What? What are you blathering about?" Sasha asked, curious.

Without answering, Tsilke sprang toward Sasha, made as though to kiss him, but instead of kissing him she bit his neck.

He held back a cry, whether of pain or of joy.

She ran off, barefoot, and he gave chase, thinking: "The forest, the forest is awakening. . ."

As she ran, her bare legs caught the dappled light of half-shaded woodland paths.

She ran off far ahead of Sasha and did not stop teasing him:

"You didn't catch me . . ."

Sasha was no longer following her. He had stopped in his tracks, observing her from afar. Since the summer she had grown more mature and beautiful. Her light hair had become a little darker, her eyes seemed deeper, more probing. Her eyes . . . in the shadows they changed from gray to blue, and Sasha did not know if there was a word to describe them, their color changed constantly.

Tsilke stood in front of Sasha, not wanting to approach. Her gaze was somehow strange.

"What? You've never seen me before, Tsilke?"

Tsilke replied, "I often ask myself what you're doing here in the forest. What brings you here? *Who* brings you here? And how long will you keep coming?"

"What are you talking about? You don't need to think about anything, you should be just like the forest, that's how you need to be. . ."

"The Forest thinks too, the forest sighs often. Maybe others don't hear it but I . . . it often seems to me that the forest is trying to speak, to let out a great yearning . . . and the branches stretch toward you like hands . . ."

Sasha took advantage of her outpouring and sprang forward, kissing her . . .

For the first time Sasha felt that his kiss stirred something deep inside her: she trembled and fell toward him. Her breath filled his face, her eyes begged for something and at the same time they burned with the wicked fire of a wild animal.

They heard a cough nearby. The road watchman was passing: "Ivan!"

He listened to Sasha's orders to hitch up the horse, and went to carry them out.

Sasha and Tsilke walked behind him: he brought them news from the city. The Luries had gone abroad. Their house was empty. Only an old maid stayed behind, and Sasha decided that he would now stay in the forest until the end of the summer.

They arrived home to find Iser eating in silence. Tsilke was sincerely glad to see her father. He was in good spirits and was more talkative than usual, but Tsilke's eyes widened when she heard what he had to say:

"You know," he said, addressing everyone, "You know that we have sold the forest." By "we" he was referring to the Company Lurie. "We've sold the forest and soon they'll start to cut it down."

"Tsilke, Nikhe and I, all of us will move away from here, away from the stream, from the road watchman, from Mistebove."

"We'll move to Svislotsh, where old man Lurie owns more woodlands."

Sasha stood by the door; he was strangely intimidated by the silent Iser. Tsilke was devastated by her father's news and Sasha felt for her.

"Reb Iser," he said, "If I ask my father, perhaps he will leave the forest be."

"The forest has already been sold, it's too late," Iser said, almost smiling.

He was a little surprised to hear Sasha suddenly taking an interest in his father's woods.

Then Iser took out a book and soon became engrossed in it: he seemed to forget all about his daughter, forgetting that he had a boss, old-man Lurie who was on holiday in Karlsbad and that Lurie had a son, Sasha, a good-for-nothing who came to visit now every couple of days for who knows what reason . . .

Her father's silence unsettled Tsilke and at the same time it felt almost like approval. Tsilke and Sasha went off into the woods. Aunt Nikhe went to the stream to scrub the dishes.

Walking alongside Sasha, Tsilke suddenly started to smile and laugh lightly. . .

"What is it, Tsilke?"

"Nothing," she replied, laughing all the more. And Sasha was even more confused when she fell on him a second time and gave him another kiss followed by a bite. . .

The hours passed in playful joy. They rejoiced in every little thing. If they happened upon a berry they would bite into it with a kiss. . . but suddenly they remembered that Tsilke's silent father was sitting at home.

They walked back slowly. Iser was gone, he had already left.

"Was he angry?" Tsilke asked her aunt.

"When is he ever *not* angry?" He's gone to Svislotsh for a couple of weeks . . .

Tsilke looked at the wall. His tefillin were gone, a sure sign he would not be back for some time. Her heart rejoiced, and Sasha broke out suddenly into song. He remembered a song from the mountain people. Tsilke imitated him and the dishes fell out of aunt Nikhe's hands . . .

6
Late Summer

IN MISTEBOVE, meanwhile, there was much to talk about: young Lurie, the foreigner, was on everyone's lips.

"And if you have a rich father, I suppose you can get away with anything."

"Settled himself down there in the forest with the helpless girl."

"It'll end in tears, mark my words, it'll all end in tears!"

"Poor old Iser, his only child . . ."

"It's his own fault, it's all his fault: why did he go to Svislotsh leaving his daughter with Lurie's son?"

And when aunt Nikhe came into town to buy food the curious townsfolk gathered around her:

"What news from the woods? Is *he* still there? Yes. And Tsilke? Let's hope nothing bad happens."

Nikhe would open her eyes wide, as though only now realizing how imminent the danger was. And she would hurry home, without answering anyone.

The girls of Mistebove would follow her with curious eyes:

"The old woman knows everything, but she doesn't want to tell us, she's silent like a witch."

People whispered and spoke openly that Lurie's son was having a love affair with Tsilke.

Froyke would prick up his ears, catching a word here and there. An impotent rage tormented him:

If it wasn't for that Lurie, Tsilke would never have run away from him, Tsilke wouldn't have pushed him away. He'd been so blind. Earlier he hadn't even noticed, she was a girl like all the other girls, a little wild, a little quiet . . .

But now she'd grown up so slender and beautiful that even Lurie, the rich boy from the big city, couldn't bring himself to leave the forest anymore.

And the forest . . .

The forest had grown older, more silent. When the day was over a black sheet, strewn with golden dots, covered everything and all the sounds and notes, all the sighs of the forest rolled up into one great silent hush . . .

The breeze there still had a few untold secrets. A half-dead beetle scrambled up the bark of a pine. The beetle was black, the night was black, and the black sheet with its golden points was so very far away.

Afterwards the darkness receded and, in the pallor of the new morning, the tips of the trees began to peek out,

each tree gradually drawing away from its neighbor—
enough kissing in the darkness. Each tree returned to its
post from the previous day, standing to attention like a
soldier, and began casting shadows.

But if the trees were silent, the squirrels and the birds
spoke up in their place. The last butterflies of summer
meandered among the trees—they had left the fields for
nothing; there was less sunlight here.

Which of God's fine creatures cared what was happening in the forest?

The sun still shone by day and, wherever it found a
place free from shadow, it concentrated all its beams and
drew out young blades of grass from the earth just as it
had done in early spring.

Yet somewhere there was already an empty nest and
from time to time an abandoned feather floated out of it,
along with a few dried-up pieces of eggshell. Threads of
spiderwebs hung in the air, hanging and tangling themselves between the branches until the wind tore them
free and left them to snake in the currents of air.

The night moved onward, leaving behind its great silence in the illuminated forest. With each passing day
the silence grew deeper and more earnest. Birds ceased
their song abruptly. The crickets were rarely heard. Only
the squirrel with its catlike cry broke ranks and ignored
the forest's restraint, its cry ringing out more clearly and

wilder than before . . . sounding for all the world like an alarm, a call to arms.

By this time Sasha had spent several weeks in the woods. He could not and did not want to leave. It had happened. He already felt that he would not escape. Life had grabbed hold of him with firm, branch-like arms and held him fast . . . Tsilke was his . . .

He experienced moments of clarity where he would resolve to escape, but at the same time he knew he would not survive if she did not belong to him. She would run to meet him, not leaving his side for a moment. Her lips were drawn to his, her arms embraced him . . . She'd always been a girl of few words—she seldom spoke but her eyes gazed ever deeper and deeper into his. Wordless kisses and occasional laughter. She laughed softly, timidly, and it seemed as though she were teasing him . . .

Once she came out with the following words:

"Why don't you kiss me the way Froyke kissed his gypsy girl?"

"Who's Froyke? What gypsy girl?" Sasha wondered.

And she told him all about the scene she'd witnessed recently in the forest.

Sasha grew pensive. Deep down he was a little ashamed before the forest girl . . . but she would not allow him ruminate for long, and he was taken aback when she said:

"You'll never leave, we'll stay together right here in the forest."

"It won't be long before they cut down the whole forest, Tsilke!"

"Then we'll move to Svislotsh."

"Is that what you reckon?"

"Yes, yes yes," and she accompanied each "yes" with a kiss. He saw what was happening to her: a life had awoken, a flame, a hidden fire had been lit, and he was being ever more dazzled and entangled. He thought and thought . . .

Until in the end he stopped thinking altogether.

Day and night flowed into each other. His whole life unravelled before him: his time abroad, his worldview, his lethargic inertia. He opened his arms, opened his heart wide and exhaled, releasing it all into the forest, into the world. Days and nights passed, moments of passion and oblivion. It used to bother him that Tsilke understood him so little, that he had to adapt himself to her, choosing his words carefully. But now it no longer seemed necessary; all that was needed was to gaze deeper and deeper into each other's eyes, to sink their teeth into each other as they kissed—that was the best language, the most important and the most sacred . . .

And Tsilke bit with ravenous, unexpected ferocity. As though she had the sharp incisors of a squirrel and was now using them on Sasha's lips, on his neck . . . He would indeed try to defend himself from her, like a bear defending itself against a more agile predator. He tried to pacify her, with a gentle touch and an avuncular smile, until he too would abandon himself and bite her in return . . .

Iser was in the Svislotsh forests the whole time. Nikhe sighed, and her sighs grew heavier and increasingly apprehensive.

The smitten Tsilke learned to fool the old woman: she would go to bed at night and wait for her aunt—gray hair peeking out from under her wig—to fall asleep. Then she would slip back into her dress and run to the other cabin, to Sasha . . .

He would wait for her, and if the night was warm they would spend it in the woods.

The only sound was the stream swirling over the stones and speaking in its inscrutable water-language. Sometimes branches would begin to rustle lightly, as something disturbed them in their forest-dream.

Tsilke and Sasha slept in the woods among the trees, slumbering as soundly as the dead, until the woodsmen would come with their sharp hatchets. A breeze passed and it knew the secrets of all the living and the dead.

Tsilke snuggled up to Sasha, telling him whatever thoughts came into her head. She had now become talkative, asking Sasha about everything, as if she had been born anew. She wanted Sasha to tell her what the city was like, what the people were like there.

Once, in a moment where their arms had just released each other and Sasha gathered a thick bundle of her hair in his hand, she asked him:

"Sasha, are all people like this?"

"Like what?"

"Like us," she said, in a fit of laughter, and started to kiss him again, and her wriggling body fell against his. The forest itself listened as she murmured softly with each ardent kiss: "Like this, like this, like this . . ." And the murmur drifted off somewhere, falling on the trees like velvet, like silk, warming the air . . .

"Like this!"

Afterwards she fell asleep by his side, among the trees which had witnessed her first steps, and her first laugh. But Sasha was an outsider, a stranger from Grodno. He came from abroad with many suppressed doubts and desires.

He was deep in thought, Tsilke's words still ringing in his ears. Yes, the whole world was *like this*. Unfamiliar feelings fought within him until dawn. One the one hand he was proud that Tsilke, such a lively child of nature, had fallen into his grasp; on the other hand he was starting to feel as though he was the one bound to her. He felt a great restlessness, but he shook it off; he did not like to dwell on painful thoughts.

There she was, sleeping peacefully—no doubt dreaming of the daytime forest—what has she seen in her life?

Then dawn came and Sasha could once again gaze at her face, which the night had made so pale, and in that moment he felt a deep affection for her, an almost paternal compassion. He would never leave her, he would protect her from life's hardships. This is what he thought in that happy moment . . .

And by day . . .

Sasha's gray hat was always lying around, either in the forest, or in the house. He never wore it. Aunt Nikhe prepared food with trembling hands, with uneasy glances. Several times, she'd considered sending Shleyme to find Iser in Svislotsh and tell him that Sasha was still in the forest, not leaving Tsilke's side, and that no good would come of it.

She did not yet know about the nights when Tsilke snuck out of the house.

One time, Sasha announced that he would like to return to Grodno for a day; there was no one at home, and perhaps some letters had arrived for him.

Tsilke went pale. She felt threatened by the city, and the letters he was waiting for. As soon as a thought entered her mind, she put it into words:

"If you go away I'm afraid you'll never come back."

"Where would you get that idea, foolish child." This girl, it seemed, would never let him go. He became even more afraid of Tsilke and retreated into himself, feeling a momentary flash of anger before deciding not to go. Tsilke was glad.

Later that night she came to him with a question that greatly troubled him:

"Sasha, If I have a child, will it be a bastard?"

He did not know how to respond. He wanted to change the subject, to avoid the question, but she persisted.

"In Prudne, I saw them beat the shepherd's daughter, because she was going to give birth to a bastard."

Sasha was torn; he had no answer for her. The stark reality of life struck him in that short question: "What's going to happen?" And when he saw that Tsilke's face grew sad, he pressed her to him and said reassuringly:

"Kid, no one's going to beat you. I won't let them insult you, everything is going to be fine."

Later, when he found himself alone for a moment, he took a stroll into the forest and thought, considering his situation. It all seemed so awfully strange, so awkwardly terrible; he had led himself into this, he who had always run away from life's complications, not allowing himself to be conquered. Now the matter had grabbed him, binding him hand and foot, because . . .

Tsilke was not like—could never be like—all the previous women he had encountered, out there abroad, they had not wanted much from him, nor he from them. Brief relationships, brief passions, with no strings attached. But Tsilke was a lonesome orphan. Iser was an employee of Sasha's family and had already spoken with him; there had been tears in the quiet old man's eyes.

Sasha wandered with slow steps deeper and deeper into the forest. He reflected on his lonely life, chiding himself for his laziness and how ill-suited he was for life. He was young, his thirtieth birthday still a good few years ahead of him, and yet he had already outwitted everyone, ridiculed everything. And Tsilke? What feelings did he have for her? Was it love or merely passion? He could not give a full reckoning. Most likely it was no more than the thrill of discovering a rare, untouched specimen and being dazzled.

Tsilke's image came to him. He tried to compare her to all the women he had ever met. He exaggerated and diminished her beauty, her youthful fire, which had lit him up. He asked himself frankly, would he be capable now of going out into the world, and forgetting her? He felt an unfamiliar yearning take hold of his whole being . . . Maybe it really was love? He had never felt anything like it before.

What's going to happen? What's going to happen?

He looked around at the forest. A great calm lay in the trees around and above him; rays of light trickled wearily down to the forest floor while birds sang somewhere in the distance.

He would have liked to take that calm into his heart—thinking was making him tired. He could not suffer and did not wish to suffer.

Suddenly, he heard his name. Tsilke was calling him, clapping her hands and shouting: "Sasha!"

He called back and they set off together back to the house. She laughed, unaware that Sasha was troubled. Her laughter surrendered to him. He grabbed her hand and led her away into the forest. At first she resisted, then she closed her eyes and her breathing began to quicken. He ran his fingers over the thin fabric of Tsilke's dress, feeling her body underneath and his whole being was aflame. The green trees shimmered in his eyes, the beams of sunlight flickering between them. They took a few more steps and then fell together to the ground.

All alone, far from other people, as long as the bird singing on the branch does not give them away.

Afterwards, when Tsilke opened her eyes—eyes which reflected the green of the forest, she said to Sasha.

"You? I . . . for a moment there I thought it was Froyke."

"Froyke? What does he have to do with anything?

But Tsilke did not know what to say. This had happened to her many times: whenever Sasha lit up and kissed her with such passion, whenever he held her so capably and easily in his arms, she pictured Froyke Barash, whom she had always been afraid of . . . because he'd always wanted to kiss her, and now the same thing had happened to her again. She opened her eyes, looked at Sasha and saw Froyke, in his disheveled black shirt, looking back at her with a menacing smile.

Sasha was completely bewildered. Tsilke once again reached out her hand to him, laughed and joked until the sun had transported itself to another part of the forest. The tree they were sitting under began to slowly bleed drops of resin, like great tears of amber, drawn out by the rays of the setting sun.

They walked back. Sasha had forgotten everything he'd been thinking about. Tsilke laughed, and her laughter lightened his mood. Every now and then he opened his eyes wide to admire how she hopped around without a care in the world.

Nikhe would prepare them food, but she kept her distance. Deep down she was still angry with them. She had no evidence, but she was convinced that they had sinned nonetheless. She was powerless; there was nothing she could do, so she put all her faith in God. She had only one glimmer of hope: summer was coming to an end and Sasha would not stay in the forest for much longer.

Days went by, dry and hearty, while the nights were deathly silent. And on one of those nights, Aunt Nikhe heard a rustle inside the room. She soon drifted back to sleep, but it was an uneasy sleep, lasting only a short while. She opened her eyes, looked around in the dark, and called out:

"Tsilke."

No response. Nikhe got up and lit the lamp . . . Tsilke was not there; her bed was empty and unmade. The old woman turned pale with fright . . . She ran to the door and called out again, "Tsilke." It was night in the forest and the night did not respond.

In that instant Nikhe wanted to know everything, to get to the bottom of it all. She was filled with rage and suspicion. Tsilke, whom she'd raised like her own child, that same Tsilke was taking her for a fool—sneaking out of the house in the middle of the night . . . Nikhe went out into the woods and walked a few paces to the left, a few paces to the right. The night was too cold for her old bones, and she shivered. The breeze tugged at her gray hair. She no longer called out to Tsilke, no, no, she wanted to see for herself. She wanted to know if the sin had already been committed. She crept like a conspirator towards the stream. The water was following its usual path, babbling restlessly. The night seemed so mute to the old woman, so packed with terror. During the day she had never felt her age like she did now in the dark among the trees. She forgot for a moment about Tsilke and thought about her own life, about her many lonely years, and she felt that the graveyard was not so far, not so very far at all. Who had she lived for, and who would cry for her once she was gone?

Tsilke . . .

Nikhe had given her heart and soul for her and now here she was sneaking out at night to lie in sin.

There was no sign of them in the forest. Maybe they'd gone further. The old woman had no energy to continue, and she could barely see. Then, just as she was about to turn back, she heard Tsilke's muffled laughter. Nikhe shuddered. The laughter was coming from Sasha's room, from the other cabin.

She crept closer and stood for a few moments under the window, stood and shuddered at every noise she heard—everything was clear. There was no more doubt, and the night became twice as dark for her, her legs were weak. She wanted to go back, but heard Tsilke's laugh again. She could not hold back any longer and started knocking at the window shouting: "Tsilke, Tsilke, Tsilke!"

The room fell silent. The whole forest, the whole world held its breath. The old woman went back to her house, collapsing on her bed with a groan. In the forest, it seemed as though thousands of voices were pouring in, calling out: "Tsilke, Tsilke." The voices ran through every dark corner, latching on to every branch. The noises fell into the stream and the currents carried them away together with pieces of the night.

Aunt Nikhe wept into her pillow. Responsibility for the sin fell on her and her alone. She should never have left Tsilke out of her sight. She should have driven Sasha out of the forest—like a crow that croaks too long by the window, like a dog.

Later, she heard the door open. She listened as Tsilke crept back in and crawled into bed. The room was dark. Neither woman said a word. One who had lived such a pious life, and the other who had begun to live her life in sin.

Over in his room, Sasha was left alone. The cry of "Tsilke," which had ripped through the night banished any hope of sleep.

Nikhe had been the one to call out, but it seemed to him that the night itself was shouting at him. The wicked night would not let him sleep. He began to smoke one cigarette after another. He went over to the window and looked out into the darkness.

"What's going to happen?"

At one moment it all seemed so simple: in the morning he would go to the road watchman, Ivan and tell him to saddle up the horse. He would leave the forest and go far away.

"No, that will never happen." He decided a minute later, and suddenly felt such a yearning for Tsilke who had been so scared when Aunt Nikhe had knocked on the dark window. What is she doing right now? Crying no doubt, while her aunt curses and punishes her.

Sasha jumped from one thought to the next. His head burned with excitement. He began to feel like a criminal, and wanted to think up a fitting punishment for himself, one he deserved.

He trembled several times, imagining the forest was calling again, "Tsilke, Tsilke!" The room still held traces of Tsilke's warmth. The scent of the woods from her hair still pursued him. He felt both good and bad in that moment. And suddenly the old carefree Sasha Lurie stirred inside him.

"So be it!" He said to himself and soon drifted off to sleep.

The first thing Sasha heard the following morning, as sunlight streamed into his cabin, was the sound of Tsilke's singing. He went over to the window and saw her in the distance. She was washing clothes in the stream.

There she was, singing . . .

The previous night, with Nikhe's voice echoing in the darkness, seemed like a bad dream. The forest was so sunny, and when the sun shone, all worries seemed smaller; its rays reached into the darkest corners of one's soul, making sadness impossible, forcing you to believe in something.

Sasha promptly washed, dressed, and went out into the forest. He approached from the side; Tsilke did not notice him. She was beating the laundry, occasionally breaking into song, starting and stopping. Her voice carried far into the woods, rising above the tips of the trees and suddenly breaking off with the echo.

Lurie's son had hatched a plan, and with hasty strides he headed back to Iser's house.

Nikhe was working, it seemed she had been crying. Sasha came closer.

"Nikhe! Listen, Aunt Nikhe, I need you, I need your help today."

Nikhe did not look at him, asking coldly:

"What?"

"Aunt nikhe, There's a rabbi in Mistebove, isn't there?"

She looked at him, astonished.

"There's a rabbi, yes. What do you need a rabbi for?"

"Listen, Aunt Nikhe, if you'll help me, I'll arrange everything myself, it must happen this very day."

"What are you talking about? I don't understand."

"I want to marry Tsilke. You hear me, Aunt Nikhe, it must happen today."

Aunt Nikhe was so dumbfounded she stared at Sasha and dropped what she was holding. Both fear and joy awoke inside her.

"Why the rush, without a father, without guests?"

Sasha did not let her finish.

"There's no time to waste, Go straight to Mistebove, talk to the rabbi and have him prepare everything. We'll be there this afternoon."

"I'll send Shleyme to Svislotsh to bring Iser back—he's the girl's father after all," Nikhe said.

"There's no need to send for anyone," Sasha said sternly. "You love Tsilke, don't you? This is about her happiness . . . Later it might be too late."

She stared at him with wide, weary eyes and tucked her gray hair under her wig.

She did not move, so Sasha took her by the hand, and led her to the chest where she kept her shawl.

"Take your shawl and go to Mistebove!"

She obeyed. But first she went to find Shleyme at the distillery. She wanted to send him to Svislotsh to fetch Iser, but Shleyme was not there. She stood for a moment and hesitated before setting off for Mistebove herself, littering the path with her sighs.

In the meantime, Sasha went to Tsilke.

"Good morning!"

But instead of responding she plunged the washboard into the water, splashing Sasha from head to foot, and went back to work.

"Did your Aunt say anything to you last night?"

"No!"

"What did she do?"

"She cried . . ."

"And you?"

"I went to sleep."

In that moment Sasha thought that she'd taken the whole thing in her stride a lot easier than he had. She'd gone straight to sleep, while he'd been tormenting himself by the window.

"Tsilke, do you own a nice dress?"

"Yes, why?"

"And shoes?"

"I have shoes too. My father brought me some not long ago. But why are you asking?"

"We're going to Mistebove . . ."

"What?" She put down the washboard and went over to Sasha who was standing by the water's edge, smoking. "And what are we going to do in Mistebove?"

"We're going to the rabbi, to get married."

She through her wet arms around Sasha and shrieked; giggling and hopping up and down, she almost knocked them both into the stream.

She was delighted by the idea of going somewhere, delighted that there would be a commotion, that it would be lively. She took no notice of the gravity of the moment. Sasha saw this and it endeared her to him all the more.

Suddenly she broke the silence.

"But why shoes? In summer, I walk to Mistebove barefoot, always barefoot."

Sasha convinced her she should wear shoes because it "just wouldn't do," even though deep down he thought it would be very original if she stood under the wedding canopy in bare feet.

Then, when Tsilke resumed her work, she thought about the matter in more detail and began bombarding Sasha with questions:

"What's my father going to say? Or *your* father? We haven't asked anyone?"

Sasha reassured her:

"And what about yesterday, and the day before yesterday when we were kissing in the woods the whole time? We didn't need anyone's permission then either."

"True, we didn't ask anyone; we're not children after all . . ."

She ran her hands provocatively over her dress, smoothing the creases, and posed proudly in front of Sasha, in front of the whole forest. Sasha noted again how much she had matured, how much she'd grown.

We're not children after all—the phrase rang in his ears. He eyed her with enthusiasm.

"Don't just stand there ogling; kiss me!"

But when he tried to kiss her, she bolted and would not allow herself to be caught.

She ran and he gave chase, while the forest listened in on their laughter. The laundry was abandoned back by the stream. Far off in the forest, Sasha caught her and paid up her debt of kisses, with interest.

Afterward, she went inside to prepare her shoes and dress. Sasha was left alone.

He thought . . .

He thought that what he was about to do, must be done. Of all the questions swimming around in his head, he understood one thing for certain: You can't leave someone like Tsilke . . . It must be done as soon as possible; that very day, they had to erect a wedding canopy. Perhaps he was afraid of himself. What if he got cold feet, or other things got in the way that would hinder him from taking responsibility.

Just then, he saw, among the trees, someone new: it was a middle-aged Jew with wrinkled clothes, and a dented bowler hat. He approached Sasha slowly.

"*Sholem-aleykhem*, *Mazl-tov!*" and he extended his hand. Sasha shook his hand, and regarded him with a curious stare, as if to say: *Who are you and what do you want?*

"I'm the Mistebove rabbi's shammes," the man introduced himself.

And Sasha had the impression that a messenger from another world had paid him a visit.

"Everything is prepared," the man continued. "The old woman Nikhe is waiting for you; if you like we can go there now."

Sasha told the man to go to the road watchman Ivan, to tell him to saddle up the horse right away. The man did so without delay.

And there on the porch stood Tsilke, in her white dress, wearing shoes which didn't really suit the usually barefoot girl.

She seemed taller and slimmer. A shy smile lay on her face. While she had gotten dressed, she'd had time to think things over. There was a charming earnestness in her eyes. She looked around, examined the forest from every angle, as though she were saying goodbye to her only acquaintances, the trees.

Sasha noticed her and approached. *Her eyes are blue again today.* He thought. *Strange, how her eyes change color, they often turn from gray to blue.*

"Tsilke, the shammes has come from Mistebove. Your aunt is waiting for us there. I sent him to Ivan to fetch the carriage."

She went to him and lay her head on his chest, before looking up into his eyes.

A world of translucent blue, a good-natured soul, gazed into his eyes and touched the very cords of his soul. That moment was the first time in his life that Sasha had ever been so deeply moved. His heart pounded.

She was his. She gave herself over to him like a child, and in return for that trust he would do her no harm. In truth, he possessed his own kind of decency. He often thought that he would prefer not to get his hands dirty . . . He'd been a little indecent on occasion, but nothing that couldn't be scrubbed clean if needs be . . .

Tsilke thought for a moment and asked:

"Do you really want to marry me?"

"Yes, kid, I'm absolutely sure."

"And you won't have any regrets?"

Sasha's heart pounded hearing such a question, a question that so efficiently hit its mark, but he had already decided that today he would refrain from any soul-searching. There would be time for that later in the city. He answered Tsilke with a kiss, and that reassured her.

Ivan and the shammes arrived with the carriage.

All four of them mounted the carriage and they set off. There were empty fields nearby, entirely bathed in sunlight, all surrounded in woodlands.

Tsilke forgot everything. The sun and the brightness took hold of her. She shouted at the horse, "Giddyup!" and broke into song several times. Sasha agreed with the shammes that they should avoid a commotion in the village. Only those who had to be there should know anything about the wedding.

The carriage came to a stop not far from the village. The shammes walked ahead. Tsilke and Sasha followed him. They followed the strange man as if they were lost. Tsilke found it hard to walk in her shoes; she'd been going barefoot for so long.

Later, they sat in a narrow room, where about a dozen people had gathered, invited by Aunt Nikhe. Nikhe sighed constantly, but in her sighs she understood one thing: If there had been an accident, Sasha could make amends now under the wedding canopy.

The rabbi asked Sasha something, and noted down the response in a large ledger. Then they carried a piece of embroidered cloth with four poles out into the yard.

They asked Sasha to say something, handed him a ring, and a goblet of wine. However serious and preoccupied he was in that moment, several times he felt like laughing: *What do they want, all these people?*

But he soon snapped out of it and thought: *This is necessary, this is necessary. Just a few more minutes and I can be rid of them.*

Afterwards the people began to drone like buzzing insects:

"*Mazl-tov, Mazl-tov, Mazl-tov*!"

Tsilke crossed her arms miserably and looked at the people. Aunt Nikhe cried and kissed Tsilke repeatedly.

A man approached Sasha and began to speak:

"The Luries, a lineage like that is no trifle!"

Sasha handed him a paper ten-ruble note and the man stepped aside. Soon another appeared.

"Your father . . ."

Sasha gave the second man a coin and he too stepped aside. The third man approached with a smile on his face:

"The bride was no fool . . . Haha . . ."

Suddenly he found himself surrounded by so many outstretched hands: a shammes, and undershammes, another assistant shammes . . .

Mazl-tov after *Mazl-tov*, each one costing Sasha a coin. Some girls found out about the whole thing, about everything that was happening at the rabbi's place. They came running, and Tsilke stood on the threshold of the adjacent room and spoke with them. Aunt Nikhe whispered something to the rabbi and Sasha was left to sit alone for a few moments, on an old-fashioned white armchair.

He had suddenly become smaller, in stature and in his entire being. He smiled inwardly: it seemed they had cast him aside.

Bearded men poked their heads in from the next room. Nikhe had stopped whispering to the rabbi. In conversation with her friends, Tsilke let out a laugh and Sasha snapped out of his reverie . . .

He approached Nikhe:

"Now then, Aunt Nikhe, you won't need to cry anymore and have no reason to be angry with me."

At which point she burst into a flood of tears. It was several minutes before she calmed down.

Now Tsilke also felt like crying. She thought it was what was expected of her. But Sasha had already sent the shammes to fetch Ivan, who was parked in the carriage just outside the town.

By the time they left the rabbi's house a crowd of curious bystanders had gathered. Who could have kept such a thing secret?

"Lurie's son has married Iser's Tsilke."

"A barefoot girl has married the *foreigner*."

"He's obviously gone mad."

But there were people on hand to take Tsilke's side.

"The city girls can't compare to her."

"She's so beautiful, like a princess."

Sasha was relieved when the carriage finally started to move. He had nothing against the people—by all means let them amuse themselves—but he wanted to be as far away from them as possible.

There were open fields already. They went on. Aunt Nikhe was still wiping her eyes. Tsilke held on to her to stop her from falling. She had something to ask Sasha, but she was reticent. She couldn't hold back any longer and asked. after all:

"Sasha, when will our wedding be?"

Sasha laughed; he understood what she meant: for her a wedding meant music, dancing and a feast . . .

We'll have one later, kid, later."

And Ivan, the road watchman demanded his part:

"Barin, when will we have a little schnapps? A Mazl-tov like that, taking such a pretty girl away from us."

And that "pretty girl" could not sit still on the carriage.

She had already snatched up a whole bouquet's worth of wild-flowers from the side of the road. The few miles went by quickly.

As they reached the forest the sun was already burning its last fire. Many, formless flames fell on the trees, lying wriggling in death throes across their trunks.

Dusk was approaching. Everything grew dark. The evening with its eternal descended upon them . . . and Tsilke too felt the muteness around, but she did not want to worry, not even for an instant.

As the carriage came to a halt she ran to Sasha and began to shake him, laughing:

"Married, are we really married?"

Sasha calmly stroked her hair, lost in thought. The tumult around the marriage had left him somewhat disconcerted, but he was in a festive mood nonetheless.

Festive and melancholy.

The young people of Mistebove did not go to bed until very late that evening. The event had come as a surprise to them, and set them to dreaming.

"Would you hear the likes of that in a storybook?"

"And what will the silent Iser have to say about all this?"

"And what will the Luries say?"

"She'll be living the high-life now, that Tsilke . . ."

"Who knows—It's no equal match after all . . ."

Only one person kept his distance from all the gossip— Froyke. He left the village and twice set off in the direction of the forest, where the three cabins stood, but both times he turned back before he got there.

A few days later Froyke hitched his father's horse up to the carriage and set off for Volkovisk.

He did not come back. A week passed.

Old man Barash went to find him only to discover that Froyke had sold the horse and carriage, and drank away all the money—he was still drunk when Barash found him. Froyke refused to come home.

All this was on account of Tsilke—that's what they were saying in Mistebove.

7
The Forest is Felled

ON QUIET DAYS it was enough to strain one's ear to hear the axes at work. The forest was being cut down, the noise moving ever closer and closer.

Everyone in Iser's house knew that their forest's days were numbered. It was a few short months until autumn when more workers were due to arrive; the trees would be richer in resin then, making them easier to cut them down.

Summer had come to an end.

While the forest was governed by greenery as before, and the last remaining summer breezes still blew between the trees, autumn had already arrived in the fields. The yellow leaves of each deciduous tree sent the signal far and wide: something was dying, something had already died.

By the road watchman's cabin there was a small patch of guelder-rose bushes. The flowers had opened up, a charming sight . . . Everything around was green. The trees radiated green from every angle, and amid that valley of green the red of the guelder-rose berries stood out with whimsical joy.

Sasha was fond of that particular spot. He came there often, with Tsilke or on his own. He would go there to reflect, to think about himself and about the forest girl with whom he'd gone to the rabbi of Mistebove.

Now he had a wife. It had happened and yet he often found himself shuddering with a sudden doubt—and what if the whole thing had been a dream? One of those pleasant dreams that set the blood on fire, after which you lie there with closed eyes and a restful soul.

No. It wasn't a dream. He needed only to wait and she would come to him, his Tsilke. She would sneak up behind him and cover his eyes with her hands.

"Tsilke?"

Silence

And again, "Tsilke!"

"Yes, yes, it's me, it's me . . ."

The word "me" rang out over the forest, over the whole world, penetrating Sasha's soul like an exhortation, like a command . . .

A good-natured one, but a command nonetheless . . .

Sasha could not leave for any length of time; Tsilke did not allow him to go to the city, as though she were afraid someone would take him away from her there. She did not give him express orders, she did not force him, but whenever the matter arose she would shut her lips and it would be a long while before she opened them again. She could be very stubborn in her own way.

This stubbornness took two forms:

Either she would constantly embrace Sasha, kissing and biting him, or she would be like a pine sapling: beautiful, adorned with lush greenness, and mute.

After much effort Sasha convinced her to let him leave for one day. He went to Svislotsh to her father, Iser. He introduced himself, not as an employer's son, but as a son-in-law.

They met in a newly built cabin in the woods. Iser had visitors so Sasha waited for a long while before getting to the point:

"Reb Iser, *Mazl-tov* is in order . . ."

Iser raised his eyes, ran his fingers through his overgrown beard and, after a few moments of silence, asked:

"What do you mean?"

"A week ago I married your daughter, Tsilke."

The old man stood frozen to the spot.

"Yes, the rabbi in Mistebove married us."

"My daughter? Iser screamed. "What? How? why?"

"Reb Iser, what's done is done, I love her, I grew fond of her. She's mine now, my wife."

In that moment it seemed that Iser had understood everything, everything Sasha had said, and everything left unsaid. He held his tongue, went to the door, and gazed long out into the forest, standing with his back to Sasha. Sasha felt very unwelcome at that moment. It was half dark in the hut, which also affected his mood.

Sasha approached his old servant and asked him obligingly:

"What's the matter, don't you approve of the match, Reb Iser?"

In his heart Iser did not hate Sasha, though he'd heard enough bad stories about him, and now here he stood in front of him with a kind, open face.

Iser offered his hand, uttered: "I accept your *mazl-tov*," and burst into tears. Sasha was taken aback. He had never seen a grown man cry before. It was as though a hundred-year-old tree had broken, or a stone had burst open of its own accord. Iser's whole body shook and large tears ran down his face, streaming over his hairy cheeks.

Sasha felt he should leave, and so he went for a walk, to explore the unfamiliar woods nearby.

When Sasha got back to the cabin, Iser approached and wordlessly kissed him. Then he asked:

"And do your parents know about this?"

"Not yet. They'll find out about it today. I'll write to them."

"Will your father be pleased?"

Sasha answered:

"My father deals in lumber . . ."

"And what does that mean?"

"Nothing. We'll come to an understanding."

Sasha returned with Iser, who could only spare one day to make the trip from Svislotsh to Prudne.

They traveled in silence.

Iser, the old Jew who had lived his life in the woods, had learned from the trees how to be silent. His wife had died a year after their marriage, taking his happiness and hope with her into the grave. He was a man who always feared that someone would force him to speak . . .

And Sasha . . .

It was rare for Sasha to look deep into another man's soul. But on this occasion he thought about Iser during the entire journey. He felt sure that a single word could cause the old man to fall apart and so he refrained from all attempts at conversation. He could not figure out if the old man was angry or if he was perhaps even a little pleased about the whole affair.

The road ran through the empty fields. Farmers were digging up the last of the potatoes; crows were scavenging in the parched cabbage fields. All around, the world was vast and empty, and the hollow emptiness made itself at home in one's heart . . .

The road was long. To be silent on one's own is much easier than to do so in another's company. Yet Sasha was at least somewhat glad he had gone to Svislotsh.

I've fulfilled an obligation, he thought. He felt that he'd become a "man with obligations": obligations toward Iser, toward Aunt Nikhe—he had obligations towards everyone now. And he had done his part, had looked everyone squarely in the eye . . . and yet, and yet . . .

He did not want to think, he refused to admit to himself that it all required tremendous effort on his part.

When Iser arrived home, Tsilke wrapped her arms around him, kissing him where before they would have greeted each other in silence. Aunt Nikhe wiped her eyes when Iser said to her:

"May fortune smile on them, Nikhe. It was fated to happen."

Then Iser and Nikhe took a walk together among the trees. She told him the whole story while he asked short questions, periodically letting out a sigh.

"It was all fated to happen like this."

"And what's Lurie going to say about the whole thing when he gets back from abroad?"

Of all the worries this one bothered him the most. Thinking about his boss made him feel somehow guilty.

On his first day home Iser informed them that this entire section of the forest was due to be felled in the autumn. They also planned to cut down the forest around Svislotsh. Absolved of his duties, Iser would then be free to retire in Mistebove with Aunt Nikhe . . .

The children would move to Grodno, he informed Aunt Nikhe.

Sasha smiled to himself. Suddenly he had become a "child." Tsilke shuddered: "Move to Grodno, among strangers?" She bit her lip and almost burst into tears.

Sasha consoled her:

"You'll be happy in Grodno; you can't live here in the forest all your life."

"Of course I can, I can, I don't need strange people."

Nevertheless Tsilke had cheered up somewhat, curious about the new life opening up before her. But once her father had gone, she pleaded with Sasha to postpone their move to the city. She did not want to abandon the forest, which would soon be cut down.

From a distance they could hear that work was progressing. Dozens of axes hacking at the trees, and suddenly, a groaning sound—they'd felled a tree, an old resident of the forest. The racket grew ever closer, the strange echo ever clearer . . .

And the closer the woodsmen got to Iser's house, the more frequently Sasha and Tsilke went to the spot where the trees were being felled.

The forest had been transformed into an enormous battlefield. Men waded, up to their knees, through the detritus of severed limbs, gouging deep wounds with sharp hatchets in the bodies of the old trees. They worked like dwarves. Then, once a tree had its bones hacked out, they would shake it in just the right way, before jumping deftly aside, lest the tree attempt a final act of vengeance on its way down.

It is both sad and compelling to watch the work—there stands a pine, calm and proud. For a hundred years it has stretched toward the sky, higher, higher, while down below, its roots delved ever deeper into the earth. It has stood there for generations like a golden sphinx encased in a green coat of lichen, and now, in the final moments of its silent existence, it radiated beauty and certainty. Its knee has already been chopped off, but its head is held high over many other trees . . .

Toward the sun, toward the cool autumn sun the tree has raised its head, bathing in brightness. Suddenly it begins to shake and its branch-ams begin to wriggle and shake along with them. The branches become disentangled and like frightened hands they try to hold on to the tree—its body. But not long after the first shake comes the terrible event.

The tree falls quickly, breaking many of its limbs on the way down. It lies there like that for a week, two weeks, until its green needles take on the color of rust—the needles will draw no more moisture. Now men go at it, hacking off the last of its limbs with sharp axes. All that remains is a long, round skeleton. Out of its wounds and knots, seep drops of its resinous blood, a tiny ant gets its feet stuck there, and cannot save itself.

And nearby the men are hard at work.

The axes have dull, nasty voices, the echo of the forest amplifies them with doubled malice:

"Forests, beware! The danger is great! Humans are sharpening ever more axes to use against you!"

Another section of forest is cleared. A new patch has opened itself up for the sun, and on the free earth the light is somehow brighter; the air, fresher.

The sun's rays have had their revenge. Until now the shadows have hindered the supremacy of the sun . . .

"Sasha, they're coming ever closer to us, the wood-cutters."

"We'll go to the city, Tsilke."

She fell silent, and, without exchanging a word, they wandered through the fallen trees. They spoke with the woodsmen. Suddenly someone shouted at them to get out of the way. A tree, an enormous tree, was about to fall to the ground.

"Make way!"

But the tree fell a little to the side, and got tangled in another tree. And there it remained, propped up by its

companion. It almost looked as though the tree was holding its head in its hands, weeping . . .

The odors of the forest and freshly sawn wood mingled in the warmed autumn breeze. It cheered the soul,
though every moment carried new sadness transported
from an unknown source.

The fact that the forest was being cut down, that the
autumn breeze was growing every cooler, and that Sasha
was talking more and more about the city and about
moving there—it all added a layer of accumulated sadness to Tsilke's soul. They often walked in silence. At first
Sasha was glad of the silence. Tsilke left him in peace to
think. Lately he had grown fond of spending time on his
own, with his own thoughts, remembering the old days
when he was, and was allowzd to be alone.

Climbing alone in the mountains, bringing with him
nothing but his own soul, and looking into it as one gazes
into a mirror.

Now . . .

The silence had gone on too long. Tsilke nibbled her
finger, a sign that she was unhappy.

"Tsilke!"

She did not respond. He tried to hug her, but she pulled
herself free and ran off. And even when he caught her, she
took her time in answering.

"Why are you angry, Tsilke?"

"Because you're being quiet, why are you so quiet?"

"I was daydreaming."

"What were you thinking about?"

Sasha found the interrogation uncomfortable. But he did his best to hide his irritation. He wanted to reassure her.

"What do you think I was thinking about?" Sasha asked, curious.

"Clearly, you once loved someone else!"

It wasn't the first time she'd shown signs of jealousy. *Women are all the same*, he thought, angrily. But he restrained himself and pulled Tsilke close to him.

"I'm not being quiet . . . You see? You hear? I'm talking right now!" And with that he began to recite the words of a Lermontov poem:

> *AWAY from the prison shade!*
> *Give me the broad daylight;*
> *Bring me a black-eyed maid,*
> *A steed dark-maned as night.*
> *First the maiden fair,*
> *Will I kiss on her ruddy lips,*
> *Then the dark steed shall bear*
> *Me, like the wind, to the steppes.*

His voice was powerful, charming, tinged with a hint of agitation. The forest listened too taken off guard to echo his words.

And Tsilke became a different person, her eyes opened wide. Sasha saw that she was captivated, and so he continued:

> *Give me a lofty palace*
> *with an arbor all around*
> *where amber grapes would ripen*
> *and the broad shade fleck the ground.*
> *Let an ever-purling fountain*
> *among marble pillars play . . .*

". . . Do you like it?"

"Yes."

"Will you come to the city? In our house I will play for you and sing."

"And when we're in the city, you won't go off with other people? Will you?"

A brief silence.

Sasha could not find an answer, it troubled him that he had to concede everything. With that question Tsilke wished to impose conditions on him, and he had never liked that. But she was dear to him and her sorrow weighed on him. He pressed her to him and mumbled affably:

"Yes, I will always stay by your side, always."

The sun now set much earlier; each evening it expired in a brief burst of red fire. Sasha and Tsilke were making their way home where Nikhe had been worrying about them. She had prepared a meal.

"For the children . . ."

Aunt Nikhe now had a heavy workload. She'd had some new dresses made for Tsilke in Mistebove, along with new undergarments and shoes. Nikhe had gone to the Mistebove twice a day to arrange it all. She was beginning to believe that everything would turn out well. Sasha had done the decent thing in the end after all: he had not run off. And he indulged Tsilke's every whim . . . If things continued like this then the orphan will have found happiness . . . And so Nikhe worked hard, preparing the best food . . . "for the children."

Meanwhile, preparations would soon need to be made for the move to Mistebove. Iser had rented one half of a house from Barash the starosta, where Iser and Nikhe would live. Life was going to be so much quieter. Tsilke's laugh and radiant face would be gone, transplanted to the city, with the Luries.

Nikhe visited Ivan the road watchman to ask him to lend a hand later when the children were gone, to help with the move.

Ivan agreed. He smiled.

"That Tsilke, just up and got married, and what a groom! The son of a millionaire . . . That Tsilke!"

"May they only be happy," Aunt Nikhe added, wary of tempting the Evil Eye.

"And the forest will be empty," she added.

"What forest? There won't be any forest left, they're cutting down the whole thing. The stream will be left bare, the road exposed, and there won't be any shade around my house anymore."

Nikhe was waiting for the children to tell her when they intended to leave. She had to start getting ready for winter in Mistebove.

But the children kept putting it off. Fine, bright days went by, without a cloud in the sky, but the stream by Iser's house had been reduced to a trickle. The river bed began to resemble a long, white sheet, with great big holes where the stones and tufts of rotting roots poked out. What remained of the stream hurried on its way, eager to leave before winter came.

"Until the rains come." That's what Tsilke and Sasha had promised each other: when the rains came Tsilke would don her new dress and new shoes, and they would go to the city.

In the meantime, Shleyme from the distillery went into the city every few days.

Sasha sent him on various errands; Shleyme brought back cigarettes, cigars and sweets for Tsilke.

Sasha remembered another duty he had neglected: He had not yet written to his parents abroad to tell them what was going on.

And so he wrote them a short, concise letter informing them of the marriage.

A week later, the response came. Old man Lurie was not in the least unhappy about the whole matter.

"I believe," he wrote, "that now you'll make something of yourself, and everything will turn out well." His mother had only added two words: "*Mazl-tov.*"

Mother is sulking, so be it.

Sasha was happy and relieved that his family finally knew everything. And when he saw Tsilke he showed her the letter . . .

"Why did your mother write only '*Mazl-tov*'? She doesn't sound very friendly. I don't want to go to the city to live with people like that. I'll stay here . . ."

It required great effort on Sasha's part to reassure Tsilke; he was forced to lie, saying his mother had shaky hands and found it difficult to hold a pen.

These were no more than brief moments of caprice and stubbornness. Brief moments . . . As before, Tsilke wore a radiant face, lighting up many shadowy corners of the forest, and of Sasha's soul. She was the youngest in the forest. She was used to everyone treating her kindly, because she had to live her life in the forest without a mother, and with a silent father. And now that someone had come along who embraced her, rousing her body and soul to life, she found herself ready to bind herself ever more closely to him. Granting ever more trust and kisses.

Sasha did not withhold his affections, though he often felt an urge to leave the forest, to return to Grodno to be free like before. At the same time he knew this was no longer an option: Tsilke had broken into his heart; she held him in her embrace. Her bright, trusting eyes followed his every step and besides . . .

There was the responsibility he had undertaken. He had decided to become a better man; this was the duty he had accepted.

Who knows where his thought might have taken him if Tsilke ever gave him time to think. But she did not; it was as though she felt it would be against her best interests.

She always appeared to shake him, kiss him, bite him, and look deep into his eyes.

"What are you thinking about? Tell me everything!"

"I was thinking about you; in Grodno I'll dress you so well . . ."

"And I'll never again go around barefoot? And the stream . . . If only we could take the stream with us to the city."

Sasha spoke up:

"Listen, Tsilke!"

"What?"

"You have to allow me to teach you some things. I'm older than you."

"And yet, I'm a better kisser than you."

Sasha had not been expecting an answer like that and he looked at her in wonder: how much insolence and audacity that naive girl had in her.

And before he knew it, she was hugging him and teasing him, putting her lips near his and pulling them away, snuggling for a while before running home.

A seamstress had arrived from Mistebove.

Sasha was left alone. "And yet, I'm a better kisser than you"—those were her words. And she was right. He recalled their nights together.

She spent every night in his cabin now. She was shy and bold simultaneously. At night she cast off her dress and groped around in the dark to find Sasha's face, Sasha's lips.

"Mine, my Sasha . . ."

"Yours, Tsilke!"

She bit him so hard he sprung to his feet and grumbled good-humoredly.

"What? You said yourself, that you're mine."

"And what of it?"

"So I'm allowed to bite you."

Like a restless wildfire she enveloped him in her arms, caressed him, kissed him, conquering his every thought, his every feeling. She had come from the depths of the forest. Her limbs had been shaped by long summers and winters; her arms were as tough as the branches of the trees. Her hair carried the scent of resin . . . Her teeth were sharp, her lips burned, her whole body was aflame . . .

Often, when Sasha awoke at dawn and the first light began pouring in the window, he would see Tsilke, sleeping soundly by his side, the pillow entirely covered by her hair, like the pelt of an animal . . .

In those moments, he was overcome by a feeling of pride and satisfaction; he believed then that he'd found an authentic way of living, that life had finally found its way to him.

He gazed benevolently at Tsilke.

And if her sleep was momentarily disturbed, she would stretch out her arms, searching for something, until her hands would come upon a thicket of her own hair. Her fingers would burrow into it and she would continue to sleep.

Wild and young, naive and bold. Sasha thought about all the things she would need to learn in the city, and it pained him. He liked the creature just the way she was: untamed.

He would often sneak out at dawn to stroll in the woods, visiting the stream, and the twin pines, where Tsilke liked to sit.

He smoked and observed the mournful trees. A shot rang out somewhere in a distant part of the forest and Sasha remembered that the hunting season was beginning. He envied those men setting off into the woods with rifles on their backs.

That's the life. An elaborate idyl took form in his fantasy, and he smiled to himself: *tedious.*

Arriving back at the three cabins, he noticed that Aunt Nikhe was also up. She was carrying a tub into the stable to feed the cow. Her dress hung on her old bones so gracelessly; her head was uncovered, and she looked older, more pitiful . . . Nikhe noticed Sasha watching her. She felt embarrassed and hurried into the stable. Once inside, she called out:

"Sasha, is the child still asleep?"

"Yes, Aunt Nikhe."

"Oh, Sasha, Sasha!" she sighed from inside the stable.

"What is it, Nikhe?"

"Soon you'll both have to leave for the city—the weather is turning—you've taken my Tsilke away and now I have nobody . . ."

He had an idea:

"Come with us, Aunt Nikhe! You'll be comfortable with us, and it would make Tsilke happy."

"No, Sasha, I'm going to live out my last years in Mistebove, I'll prepare a home for Iser, so that he can have a place to rest his weary bones for once . . . No Sashele!"

The whole conversation took place with Nikhe inside the stable, hidden from Sasha's view. He knew she would not leave the stable as long as he stood there.

So he returned to the stream, thinking and laughing to himself: *The old woman looked so funny with her head uncovered, like a plucked chicken, and she'd called him "Sashele."* He stood by the stream and smiled at the cold, rippling waters, which forged a path for themselves through the stones and old roots.

Sasha's thoughts almost drifted off in a melancholy direction, but he remembered that he'd left Tsilke behind in bed, entangled in her own hair, and the thought lured him back to the cabin.

She was still asleep. Sasha began to sing:

> *Away from the prison shade!*
> *Give me the broad daylight . . .*

But instead of the prison doors, it was Tsilke's eyes that opened. Her face buried in a mass of hair. She languidly brushed the strands aside, revealing a pair of eyes, which gazed happily at Sasha.

No, such women are only to be found on oil-paintings, where they bear the names of various legendary figures . . .

"Sasha," she said, "I dreamed that you were Froyke . . ."

Froyke . . . Again Froyke. How many times now had she mentioned his name. Sasha felt the irritation rise inside him, but he shrugged it off.

He went to her and they started to play. By now the room was bright, and her arms lit up like fragments of sun, her young breast hidden.

She opened her eyes and looked at Sasha, as though only now seeing him for the first time . . . and he looked at her, into her soul.

"What? What is it, Sasha? What are you looking at?"

"Nothing . . . noth—"

That "nothing" contained everything . . . from that "nothing" their arms became entwined and his teeth touched hers . . .

The forest exhaled . . .

Afterwards, some time later, the following conversation took place:

Tsilke said:

"Sasha, let's not go to the city, Something about it frightens me.

"But, I'll be with you. What's there to be afraid of?"

"Sasha, they're going to cut down this forest, but we could go away to another forest, and if we have children, we can allow them to live like squirrels, they'll climb on the trees, and squeal merrily . . . Sasha, Sasha, let's not go to the city . . ."

"You're still a child with childish thoughts . . ."

"I'm afraid somehow . . ."

Sasha smothered that fear with kisses, buried it in words. But he was beginning to grow weary of it. There was only so much energy he had to give, and yet deep down he felt that Tsilke was right to be afraid . . .

Why?

He had no desire for self-examination; he avoided soul-searching because it caused him to suffer, something he was not accustomed to.

Returning from the city, Shleyme knocked on the window and Sasha went out to him. He'd brought letters and the carriage to transport their belongings.

"The whole city is waiting for you to arrive, everybody is talking about your wedding . . ." said Shleyme.

The words made Sasha tremble, "city, everybody, wedding"—what business was it of theirs? He found a girl he liked, what's it to them?"

Maybe Tsilke was right, maybe it would be better if they stayed in a forest after all.

Nonsense.

And perhaps it was on account of the sunlight shining down onto the roof of Iser's house, onto the stream, that Sasha felt content, and he put all his worries aside.

"Aunt Nikhe," he called out.

She popped her head out the door, wearing a wig this time.

"What is it, child?"

Sasha broke into laughter:

"The *child* wants to eat," he said, referring to himself. "Make me something to eat, Aunt Nikhe!" And he began shouting to Tsilke that she should get dressed quickly. Tsilke responded with a song, which she had often heard in Mistebove:

> *"What does the world say, what does the world say?*
> *That women love money . . ."*

The forest, entering a delayed autumn, listened to her song, and to the far-off echoes which all come from one place.

From that condemned spot, where one tree after another was being felled.

They ate together and Aunt Nikhe told them she'd already begun packing her things to have them sent to Mistebove . . . "What will the forest be like without us, and what will we be like without the forest?"

At those words, Tsilke ran to the window and looked out at the forest:

"It's a shame to leave this place, Sasha! Look how the trees are in mourning!"

And the trees did indeed appear mournful as, just then, dark clouds began rolling in overhead, surrounding and blocking out the sun, while a sharp gust rattled the pine needles on the trees . . . The laundry hanging outside began to sway violently, billowing up like a sail before deflating again.

"Children, It's time to give some real thought to leaving! When the heavy rains start pouring down—day and night, night and day—it will be harder." said Aunt Nikhe.

But in the meantime, no rains fell. Though the clouds had already begun to gather, they seemed to be only passing though, as though they had another land in mind, another place. A murmur spread over the whole forest. Tree bowed to tree, others shook off clouds of rusted pine-needles, pine-cones and abandoned nests . . . Suddenly the eternal calm of the forest had vanished. Trees, which in summer had stood frozen to the spot, began to rustle, speaking in whispers, while the stream writhed, its waters rippling in agitation.

On one such day Tsilke put on her shoes and took her Aunt's coarse shawl. Sasha dug up his old gray hat, which he hadn't seen in many days.

Once again they went to the woodsmen. But they were surprised by the quietness which reigned all around. Usually at that time the air was filled with the sounds of axes chopping, trees groaning and falling to the ground, branches cracking. They came closer and found the woodsmen gathered together in a circle, their axes in their hands.

"What happened?"

The forest had taken a casualty. A tree had come down too quickly and one of the woodsmen had not managed to jump out of the way in time. There the body lay now, slashed to ribbons, covered in fresh foliage. Only a pair of bare legs were visible under the vegetation. Many of the fallen trees were stained with fresh blood, and the red patches filled one's soul with dread. The forest was silent, and the gathered woodsmen cross themselves without a word. Tsilke huddled next to Sasha with cold and fright . . .

A kind of evil had stolen into the forest along with the wind and death . . . But turning homewards, they did not get far before the sound of the axes resumed.

A man had died; there were other men to take his place. The forest must be razed; the forest had been sold.

When they told Nikhe about the accident she spat out three times and mumbled something under her breath: "Let's hope it's not a bad omen."

Darkness fell sooner than usual that night. The clouds had gathered ever closer; the wind did not rest. In the middle of the night there was a rain-shower and everything became gloomy . . . Tsilke slept sadly, waking several times. She said to Sasha:

"Autumn has come; you hear the forest crying? . . . You won't leave me alone, will you?"

Sasha reassured her that autumn was not so dismal in the city. In their house, large lamps were lit in the evenings. His parents and sister would soon return from abroad. They would love Tsilke and all would be well.

She felt Sasha close to her as she drifted back to sleep, and he spoke so sincerely that she believed him.

Until Aunt Nikhe came the next morning:

"Children, the rain has stopped, your things are packed . . ."

"Then it's time to go," Sasha interrupted.

"Already?" Tsilke asked wide-eyed, her heart pounding in fear.

Sasha was a good man, and yet she couldn't shake the feeling that she was being stolen away.

Nikhe hastened to prepare everything.

The weather had turned colder, but the clouds over-head—torn by the wind—let through patches of sunlight. All day the light vanished, only to reappear a moment later.

Tsilke struck a bargain: she would go, but only if they could stay in the forest for one more day. Sasha agreed, smiling. He understood perfectly well how she felt. They spent the day wandering the forest, walking along the road.

"Are they really going to cut down the whole forest? *All* the trees will be gone? And I won't be there?"

"You'll be in Grodno."

"And you'll stay by my side, always?"

Sasha's intentions were pure, but the word "always" cut him to the quick. And, to reassure himself more than anything, he repeated several times:

"Always, always. I'm yours, after all."

The next morning a hitched carriage stood ready outside Iser's house. Shleyme sat on the coachman's seat. A cold, dry wind blew. Tears ran down Aunt Nikhe's face, Tsilke's too, even the road-watchman's wife, who had come to see them off, wiped her eyes with a handkerchief.

The trees swayed, and it seemed to Tsilke they were waving her goodbye. Sasha became flustered by all the groaning and goodbyes.

"We're ready to go Shleyme, eh?"

"Giddy up!"

Tsilke began looking frantically from left to right. The horse took off, and soon her aunt, the houses and the stable vanished from view. Copper pine-trees marched past, proud and slim, as if in a parade . . .

"Sasha," she asked, "Will I never come back here?"

"The forest will be gone," he answered curtly. His own mood was dark at that moment. Tsilke wept quietly, but suddenly she lifted up her head and began speaking rapidly:

"Over there, that's the very spot where Froyke kissed the gypsy woman. Right there is where they lay, he had his boots on—she was barefoot."

Sasha looked at her. Her cheeks were still wet with tears, and here she was recalling a story like that about Froyke and a gypsy woman.

He noticed that the recollection had distracted her, cheered her up. He deliberately kept the conversation going.

"And what's he up to these days, that Froyke?"

"He's a drunkard of course, like always. Aunt Nikhe hates him, father hates him, only the girls in Mistebove like him . . ."

By then they had reached the main road, and the strong wind cut off their conversation.

Sasha sat lost in thought. The whole story of living there in the forest, his getting married—it all felt like a fable. He had swooped into the woods and slipped off with a wife.

And now he was heading back to Grodno with her, back to his father's house.

8
Priorities

AT THE LURIES . . .

Such a large house, with so many rooms. At first Tsilke thought she would get lost inside. As she entered she saw that the lamps and pictures had been wrapped in white canvas and paper; the Luries were abroad and everything was covered to keep away the dust. Sasha wanted the house to feel more cozy, and so he arranged for everything to be put in order. For several days, servants were busy cleaning, washing windows and dusting the rooms.

Tsilke wandered from one room to another, unable to find a place for herself. Sasha followed her, looking her in the eyes. He desperately wanted her to feel at home.

She missed the forest . . . Sasha could feel it, but he assumed she would eventually settle in.

She knew, she understood that this was her life now, that things were never going to be the same, but she couldn't shake the idea that, if she felt like it, she could return to forest, to Aunt Nikhe, to the stream, to the silence . . .

She had been here before of course, when she was a young girl, but the house had been completely refurbished in the meantime, and she barely recognized it. Her Aunt would often remind her of the time she ran away from the Luries, away from Grodno, wandering over barren fields. But that was a long time ago; now she was grown, she'd been to the rabbi in Mistebove, and they'd put a gold ring on her finger and brought her to the city. She wore shoes all day and her feet hurt, but she did not mention this to Sasha in case he laughed at her.

Sasha was there in the next room. He was helping with—or supervising—the rearrangement of the furniture, the dusting.

She found herself alone for a moment. She approached the window and looked out at the almost empty street outside. On the building opposite hung a sign which said: "*Damski Portnoy.*" And because Tsilke's mind was blank, the words crept into her thoughts. She said the words out loud to herself, "*Damski portnoy, damski portnoy.*" Nibbling absentmindedly on her finger like a daydreaming little girl she felt so very out of place, so filled with longing.

Her mind's eye conjured up a pine tree, then a second, and a third, until a whole forest laid itself out in front of her. The trees stood calm and slender, bearing on their shoulders a powerful tranquility. Tsilke saw herself striding among the trees . . . Where would she go today? To Prudne! To the nobleman's estate with its fine courtyard, with graveled paths and buildings adorned with carved cornices. The nobleman has a daughter who wears such pretty dresses. She lives in St. Petersburg, but in summertime she comes to Prudne, and walks along the tidy paths on the estate. She pets her dogs—which follow her—and does not say a word to anyone.

On one of Tsilke's visits to Prudne, the nobleman's daughter called her over and posed all manner of questions . . . Where was Tsilke coming from, who was she visiting? Then the nobleman's daughter asked Tsilke to wait for a moment. She disappeared into the house and emerged a moment later carrying a large canvas, along with brushes and paint. She told Tsilke to stand still and gaze into the middle-distance . . .

Tsilke did as she was asked. The nobleman's daughter painted and painted until Tsilke's legs grew tired, yet there seemed to be no end in sight . . . Tsilke was bored, and began begging for permission to leave. The nobleman's daughter burst into laughter and let Tsilke go, but only on the condition that she come back the following day. Tsilke promised to come back, but instead of keeping her word she avoided Prudne for the rest of the summer. She was afraid to return: she could not forget how stiff and sore her legs were from standing still for so long.

And now, here in Grodno, it felt as though she had once again been cornered by the nobleman's daughter, and was once again obliged to stand still and stare into the distance . . .

From Prudne she had been able to run back home to the forest. But where could she run to now? Preoccupied, she did not notice Sasha watching her . . . A heavy carriage passed on the street outside, its wheels clattering on the cobblestones. She snapped out of her reverie and saw Sasha.

"Are you unhappy, Tsilke?" He asked, adding, "You'll get used to it! Just wait, my parents will be home soon from abroad. There'll be more life in this old place then; there'll be guests."

He took her by the hand and led her into one of the other, now spotless, rooms.

An enormous mirror shone before her, and in the mirror she could see the whole room, with all its lamps and paintings. They sat down on a soft couch and Tsilke felt as though she were sinking into a pit, she burst into laughter.

"It's good to hear you laugh, Tsilke. You see, it will all be good. You'll adapt, you'll get used to our way of life. One can acquire a taste for anything, even smoking."

But Tsilke had stopped listening. She had noticed the piano in the corner, and ran over to it:

Back in Prudne, the nobleman's daughter had also owned a similar contraption, though her's was brown and this one was black. Tsilke ran her fingers over the keys, and they responded with several discordant notes. She jumped with a start, the Kozke, and looked around, as though trying to see where the notes had come from, or where they had gone. But the notes were nowhere to be found. She tapped the keys again, louder this time, with less restraint, and in that moment she forgot all about Sasha, and everything else . . . She bashed the keys and laughed at the top of her voice, in such a way that the cacophony and her laughter blended together as one.

Sasha was happy she'd found a distraction, but deep down he was growing impatient for his parents to return. He imagined that they would also look out for Tsilke, and things would be easier for her.

Because . . .

He was already tired of constantly following her around, constantly having to worry about her.

She was sad one minute and prone to anger the next; they would need to send for a seamstress, then a shoe-maker . . . All these little tasks crowded in on him, fencing off his whole being, and he yearned to breathe free of it all.

If only his parents would hurry home.

He rarely walked in the streets now; he only remembered the world at large when he heard the whistle of a train or when he read the papers. And all the things that he had previously had little to do with had become dear to him, as though he could not imagine life without them.

And then along Tsilke came to confess to him, as though it were all somehow her fault, that her feet hurt. Still not used to the city shoes, she convinced Sasha to let her take them off, and he saw that her feet were rubbed raw.

"Oh, you poor thing, Tsilke."

"Why poor?"

"Because you're a bird in a cage, aren't you, Tsilke?"

"Yes, but you said I'll get used to it . . ."

"Of course, of course . . . Everyone gets used to everything."

And . . .

It was an autumn evening. The sun set without color. Sometimes a cart would clatter past, or voices on the street would break the silence, but only for brief moments, and in that silence Sasha and Tsilke both felt as though they were in a strange castle, surrounded by strange, unfamiliar furniture. They longed for friendship and intimacy. He caressed her, cradling her in his arms, and each caress made her feel as though she were back in the forest, as though everything was taking place there.

And perhaps, Sasha thought, perhaps there was no need to worry, no need to yearn for excitement after all. Maybe he should give himself over entirely to this untamed squirrel from the woods, who had given him such sweet hours of joy there by the stream, by the twin pines.

He grew pensive.

"What are you thinking about?" he asked Tsilke. "Tell the truth!"

"What do you think of me?"

"That you've become like another person, you've tucked in your wings. You've hidden yourself away."

"Wings? I've never had any wings."

He kissed her.

"It's only a figure of speech, back in the woods you were so much livelier."

"But you said yourself, I'll grow into it . . ."

"Is that what you want?"

"I do. But will you come with me to visit the forest some time?"

"Certainly, we will travel to many places . . ."

It was getting dark, and late. In a reverie of daydreams and kisses, they fell asleep together on the soft couch.

The old maid, Shura, entered the room several times. She wanted to call them for dinner, but the "lovers" were asleep. She left the room with a shrug.

The maid did not know what was going on. "His lordship" was no doubt playing a joke when he claimed that that timid, jumpy girl was his wife.

When his parents got back from abroad there would be a scandal.

She had served the Luries most of her life, and she was as loyal to them as a faithful hound, but now she did not know what was happening.

The city was filled with gossip about the "foreigner" getting married.

"A preordained happiness, a forest warden's girl."

"He's obviously gone mad, Lurie's heir . . ."

"His father is going to jump for joy . . ."

"It's the mother I'm worried about; she's so preoccupied with status and coming from a good family. Just picture the face she'll make."

And everyone who had occasion to visit the Lurie's in those days was bombarded with questions:

"What's she like?"

"And what about Sasha? Is he content?"

Grodno had something to talk about. And anyone who passed the house would crane their neck in an attempt to catch a glimpse in through the windows.

Inside, the rooms were being cleaned; the parents were expected back any day now.

In the meantime heavy curtains were drawn across the windows of the stately home.

Tsilke too was anxious for them to return. There was something that frightened her . . . she had suddenly seen that the world was full of so many people and you needed to learn how to speak to each one of them . . .

Even the seamstress, who came into her room, wanted to interrogate her, while the old maid, Shura, looked on her with resentment and suspicion.

Only Sasha was there to comfort and reassure her.

"Try to make yourself at home; it's my father's house, which means it's also my house!" Yet Tsilke still felt out of place. She was afraid to touch the valuables, afraid to lift her feet too far off the ground as she walked.

She sat there as if in a prison. It was cold outside and besides, Sasha never brought her anywhere because the city was large: if they showed their faces, they would be followed.

The days passed, rainy, and overcast. Tsilke's complexion had quickly grown pale . . .

And in Mistebove? What was Aunt Nikhe up to there? And in Svislotsh? Her silent father, who never made a peep? . . .

Their forest was being felled, their little stream would dry up and Tsilke would never again feel the calm and tranquility she felt before.

Sasha now found himself acting as the head of the household. He would never have dreamed of such a thing before, that he would take an interest in such details. He did it for Tsilke's sake, and . . . For his own sake too; he wanted to do something to appease the worm that was eating away inside his mind.

In the city they were already saying:

"He's becoming a man, that Sashke!"

"Taking an interest in everything . . ."

"With age comes wisdom . . ."

"He's got quite the inheritance waiting for him after all . . ."

"Taken a wifey and snuggling up at home . . ."

Early one morning, while it was still dark, there was a noise in the Lurie household. Sasha and Tsilke awoke.

"What's happening?" Tsilke asked. Sasha answered calmly:

"My parents are home. Back at last."

"They'll be angry at me, won't they, Sasha?"

"Why would they be angry?"

"Because I don't belong . . ."

"Go back to sleep another while, and I'll go and tell my parents the good news."

Tsilke was left alone in the room, but she could not sleep. She could hear voices in other rooms, loud and then quieter, people shouting and then whispering. She understood that they were talking about her and she felt trapped. She looked at the window: maybe she could escape through there, and run away from these strange people? Run away, but where to? The forest was being cut down, her father was as silent as a stranger himself, and she did not want to run away from Sasha—he was so kind to her . . .

Now he was back by her side again. He sat down on the bed and stroked her hair, saying nothing until Tsilke broke the silence:

"What did your parents say? Do they know that I'm here, that I've snuck into someone else's house?"

"Tsilke, don't talk like that. It's your house now as much as it is mine or theirs. They're already fond of you, they will welcome you with open arms, you'll see."

He comforted her until it was bright outside. The day had come and Sasha left. For the first time since she had arrived he left her alone for a few hours while he went into town. Shura brought her some tea; the old maid no longer looked at Tsilke quite as angrily as before.

Tsilke combed her hair several times, staring into the mirror.

Just then the door opened and Sasha's sister, the gymnasium student Hela, ran in excitedly. Overjoyed, she began kissing Tsilke.

She spoke quickly:

"We're going to be like sisters, aren't we Tsilkele? I will love you, we'll all love you . . . We're going to be like sisters. Oh, I so wanted Sasha to get married, we all wanted it. Father is pleased and mother will come around eventually . . . Tsilkele, Tsilkele . . ."

She spoke to Tsilke in a confidential tone, as though they had always been thick as thieves, telling her everything: about her time abroad, about her gymnasium where she was rushing that very moment, because she was very late and had missed several weeks of classes.

Tsilke did not understand everything she said, but she already felt more at home.

When Hela had left, old man Lurie entered, portlier than before.

He approached Tsilke and made to give her a kiss, startling her.

"What's there to be afraid of, Kozke? I'm like a second father to you after all, you can't begrudge your father a kiss!" With that he lay his hand on her shoulder and said:

"My Sasha vanished into my woods and came back with a bird, a precious beautiful bird. Things will be good for you here with us, Tsilke . . ."

At the moment Sasha came in from the street and his father noticed he was still wearing his old gray hat.

"Now of course you'll finally get rid of that old hat. . ."

"Why now of course?"

"You're a married man now."

"Father!"

"What, Sasha?"

"Nothing . . . The hat stays."

"Well, let's not fight about it," he said in good spirits. Just then, Mrs. Lurie came in, well rested. She entered without a word and regarded everyone coldly, then she approached Tsilke and kissed her.

"You really are beautiful. Now I understand my son." She was trying her best to remain composed and resigned. But at dawn, when she had spoken with Sasha, she had let slip some angry words.

"How could you not even ask us?"

But Sasha had interrupted her, warning her that if she said one more word, he would take Tsilke and leave the house.

The old man had been pleased by Sasha's tone. It meant that he loved Iser's daughter; loving his wife was bound to make a decent man of him.

Tsilke looked at them all, and was a little frightened of them. All she wanted was for Sasha to be on her side, but he seemed to have joined theirs:

"Look alive, Tsilke," He laughed. "Hop like you did in the forest!"

"It's not so easy to hop, Sasha, there's nothing to hop on. I'll only break something."

"Don't hang your head like that."

She stood up ramrod straight, lifting her head proudly, and looked at him . . .

"Is this how you like me?"

"Yes . . . though you're frozen stiff like an effigy . . ."

"Like an effi-what? You think that just because I'm in the city I understand all your fancy words?"

He laughed heartily.

Just at that moment his mother entered, carrying a pearl necklace for Tsilke.

"You'll accept this gift from me . . ."

Madam Lurie was famous for her love of jewellry; it was a particular passion or hers. Every day people would call to offer her precious objects, gold, diamonds and pearls. She liked to buy them and swap them, and was always making a fuss over rings and earrings.

"What with Sasha and his dogs, and my wife with her pearls, I never get any peace," old man Lurie liked to joke.

Tsilke stood there with the necklace in her hand, not knowing what to do with it.

And so Mrs. Lurie stepped closer again, placed it around her neck, and pale new beams of flight fell upon Tsilke's face . . .

From then on Tsilke received many gifts. Everyone was fond of her, they hung on her every word, her every re-action. They spoiled her and she played along. Her days were filled with clothing, jewellery, accessories and ribbons. They did not quite know what to do with her hair — so much hair! How to comb it, and in what style?

Sasha's younger sister Hela spent more time with her than anyone.

"So you're a forest girl, you were born in the forest?"

"Yes," Tsilke answered.

"Tell me about the forest then."

And Tsilke would talk about her Aunt Nikhe, about Mistebove, about Prudne, but suddenly she trailed off.

There was nothing to say about the forest. There were stones and trees and silence, and through it all ran a babbling stream . . .

"And Froyke?" Hela added.

She had heard Tsilke mention the name and always asked about him:

"He must be handsome. I'd like to see him . . ."

And she would also tell Tsilke stories about school. Tsilke would listen to it all with a smile. It seemed that she had other preoccupations now, and that she was far away from it all.

From time to time the Lurie household would be visited by a curious outsider, a neighbor, or a distant relative, and seeing Tsilke, they would ask:

"So that's your daughter-in-law? She's from the forest, is she?"

In the city there was already talk of how charming she was—the "foreigner's" little wife—and of how fond the Luries were of her.

"Hit the jackpot . . ."

"An auspicious match . . ."

"But Sashke still has that old gray hat of his . . ."

"He's the type who'll soon tire of even the most beautiful wife . . ."

Grodno had much to gossip about in the long early winter evenings, but Tsilke knew nothing of all those strange people. She had suddenly been surrounded by much love and devotion, and she soon felt a strong bond with the Luries.

And Sasha . . .

He was very pleased that Tsilke was getting along so well with his family. The more time she spent with them, the less time she spent with him, and he could once again lie peacefully in the next room on a soft couch, thinking.

About what?

For the most part he actually thought about Tsilke . . .

How had it happened? How had he, Sasha, gone to a rabbi with a girl and bound himself forever?

And yet that's what happened.

And without regrets . . .

What now? Part of Tsilke's charm had been left behind in the forest, there among the trees where her echo circled three times. Barefoot, her eyes would cast so much life into the shadows . . . and that life ensnared him.

And now . . .

He had no choice but to admit that those threads, woven of the green shimmer of the pine-needles and the echoes of the forest, with the babble of the stream that knew only how to gurgle and flow . . . Those threads which had enveloped his soul like a ball of silk had been severed, vanishing along with the summer which had now passed . . .

Now he had a wife. They slept in the same bed, and she, naive as ever, had recently made a great discovery with one short phrase:

"You know," she had said to Sasha . . .

"What, my dear?"

"Kissing was better in the forest."

"Oh, you rascal!" He laughed it off, but later he realized that it was true: the kissing had been better in the forest. Back there he thought the passion would consume him.

And now? . . .

He returned to his books, old books he'd long ago forgotten and ridiculed. Anything he could get his hands on, he browsed through and read. And when he was tired of books he had another pleasure: lying in bed, staring at the wall, counting the squares on the wallpaper and smoking.

Even his father, well acquainted with his son's ways, was taken aback.

"A married man and still the same as before."

Sasha was offended, but held his tongue. He felt guilty. He knew that he was a hopeless good-for-nothing and was happy just to be left in peace.

He could hear Tsilke laughing from the next room.

"Let her laugh!"

No doubt she was rejoicing at her latest gift.

Tsilke strode around in the strange rooms and was still afraid. There were tables with crystal glassware, with vases . . . She was very careful not to knock anything, not to break anything.

Hela and Sasha's mother were teaching her how to hold a knife and fork.

She had laughed at the dining table the first time they pointed out she was holding the fork wrong. She was an attentive pupil: she only needed to hear something once and she would remember forever.

And yet, surrounded as she was with love and devotion, she was often frightened, her eyes darting in every direction. She would look at everyone sitting around her as though they were strangers and cry out:

"Where is Sasha? Where is he?"

He wasn't in their room, so she ran through the other rooms only to find him lounging on a sofa.

"Sasha, why are you on your own? Why did you run away from me?"

"Kid, I didn't run away, I like being by myself to think."

She looked at him and looked inside herself: Maybe she had done something wrong? Maybe she laughed too much? Maybe she hadn't been behaving properly? Maybe that's why Sasha was so cold and distant . . .

"Sasha," she begged him, "don't be like that . . ."

"Like what?"

She did not know how to make him understand, she stumbled over her words and became despondent.

Sasha realized he was too distant; he had grown too self-assured and forgotten his place in the world.

He had a wife, he'd been to the rabbi in Mistebove . . . Carefree Tsilke from the forest. With her firm arms and naive soul, she'd given him so much during those summer days in the woods.

And he had taken her from the forest, to the city, brought her to his relatives, and they all looked to him, imposing on him with words and with silence that Tsilke must become his priority.

Priority . . .

She was staring him in the face, reaching out to him with slim, stiff arms, speaking to him, waking him, shaking him and not leaving him a moment alone.

Making demands . . .

Love, attention, tenderness and words, words, words.

Demanding he speak, tell stories.

Often in those moments he recalled a particular mountain somewhere in Switzerland where he'd broken away from the others and gone off on his own, climbing higher and further, with only the rocks for company. And if he reached the very heights or fell down into a crevice, no one would care, no one would try to find him.

But now if he tried to go into another room for half an hour Tsilke would appear beside him.

Kind, bold, naive Tsilke.

She who had given him everything and demanded everything in return.

He wrestled with himself, each time managing to stifle his anger and impatience, and instead of losing his temper he caressed her and comforted her, until he had reassured her, and reassured himself.

It was enough to gaze into her eyes, and feel her trembling body for everything to be forgotten.

The forest came to mind again. The nights they spent together with her undone hair which still smelled of resin . . .

"I imagined, just now, that I was back in the forest."

"Me too, Tsilke."

"They're probably chopping down the trees there as we speak."

"Perhaps . . ."

"Will they cut down the twin pines too?"

"Of course."

"Aunt Nikhe misses me, no doubt. The old woman is probably crying."

"Old people enjoy a good cry."

"And my father. Sasha, why does my father never come to visit?"

"He feels like he has sinned against his employer, as though *he* had married me, not you!"

A gloomy "oh" fell from Tsilke's heart, and was lost in the darkness of the room.

Sasha pondered. Just then they heard Hela's voice:

"Tsilke, Tsilke!"

Tsilke ran to her new friend, to Hela, leaving Sasha alone.

Outside it was snowing and raining at the same time. The city seemed so small somehow; Grodno with its little shops and little people. He was sick of them all, and of his father and his mother, constantly polishing their new jewellery.

On one such evening, Sasha left the house and strolled down Soborna Street with its narrow pavement.

Suddenly he heard the clinking of billiard balls. He went into Katowska's Cukiernia, just to watch the billiard players.

And he started playing a few rounds of billiards.

"Where is Sasha?"

"At Katowska's"

"What's he doing?"

"Playing billiards . . ."

And the chalk-tipped cues, the green table with all the fives, twelves and fifteens now filled Sasha's whole day.

This had not gone unnoticed at home.

His father tried to influence him with his strongest argument:

"Sasha, why leave your young wife alone?"

"What, I should take her everywhere with me?"

"Sasha, people are laughing at us."

"And I laugh at them!"

He lit a cigar, put on his gray hat, and headed off to Katowska's once again.

"Who does he play with there? With low-lives. With a drunken functionary, with a Swiss-man from the hotel . . . Who else?"

"And for all that he had to study abroad?"

"Was it for this his whole education?"

"Having a father like his with a good name and fortune?"

"Marrying an innocent child from the forest?"

There was plenty to gossip about, and they talked. Sasha, as if to spite everyone, continued playing. His partners embraced him warmly; it's not everyday you catch a fish like that.

At home everyone was infuriated with Sasha's billiard playing, because he had abandoned Tsilke, and they hid from her the real reason for his absence. . .

He's going to work in his father's office.

Sasha confirmed it himself, when she asked him about his work.

"Yes, yes, in my father's office."

Afterwards he felt guilty: Was there any need to tell lies, to Tsilke of all people, who believes everything she's told? It troubled him greatly. The lie had debased him, made him childish, and he began to flee from home even more, and from himself . . .

The longer this went on, the more days that went by, the less that remained from the forest, from his intoxication.

Tsilke . . .

Was she still the same person?

He could not always talk to her anymore. Sometimes he had the impression he was a lot older than her.

And it made him weary:

Always having to choose the right words, to adapt to her mindset, to her whims . . .

Suddenly he felt sorry for her: what fault is it of hers? He came to her forest with kind words—and she, in her loneliness, had fallen into his arms and put all her trust in him.

He sought out the best words, caressed and kissed her, sat with her for hours. While deep inside he strained to bury the signs of his own unease and boredom.

He would sing, play piano, throw himself eagerly on Tsilke and kiss her as before, carrying her around from room to room.

His parents took some pride in their only son, for once deriving a little vicarious pleasure from him.

He grew colder, cursing Grodno and the tedious autumn in his heart. He was waiting for the opportunity, a chance to escape . . .

And he hurried to Katowska's, to play billiards.

The long cues shimmered as they cut though the shafts of light which illuminated the half-dark room. A patch of the green table shone like a meadow, and the dull clack of the heavy balls drowned out every thought, every stirring of his conscience.

Sometimes he would stay there until late at night, and Tsilke would ask the others:

"At the office so late? Why does Sasha work so hard?"

They sent someone to get him:

"Tsilke is restless."

"Ha! Tsilke? Who's she to be calling me, to be ordering me around?"—He smacked the cue on the ground and went home in a foul mood.

In the bedroom afterwards, when Tsilke asked him why he was working so late, he told her the truth:

"What office! I don't go to my father's office, I was playing billiards, do you understand?

"Billiards . . ."

He had a new task before him: Tsilke had no idea what billiards were. Grumbling and with a smirk he explained to her in detail the game with the cues, and balls, on the green table.

She took an interest, thought for a moment and began shouting at Sasha:

"Why don't you take me with you? I could play too and wouldn't have to miss you so much."

Imagine the scene, thought Sasha, a couple such as himself and Tsilke turning up at Katowska's to shoot some balls . . .

Tsilke found herself spending more and more time looking for Sasha, who went missing more and more often. Seeing that he was not there, she would hide in her room, sitting by the window, thinking.

Why had he been so kind back in the forest?

Why did he run away now?

There was already snow on the street outside, and she was reminded of winters past, of the paths she trod herself from the woods to Mistebove, the broad whiteness that lay over the surrounding fields, the closed doors in Mistebove, through which thick mist poured out, the feathers, the girls and their songs . . .

Her heart was stirred by all those memories, and she felt so claustrophobic in Grodno. They had bought her dresses and shoes, they loved her, old man Lurie often sat her on his knee and stroked her hair, speaking and laughing:

"What a forest girl my Sasha managed to scoop up in his net . . ."

"Such a rascal, who would have expected it?"

And Hela would come to her several times a day, with warm kisses.

"You know," said Hela, "you taste good. It's good to kiss you."

But Sasha was gone; he'd snuck out without saying a word to anyone.

And no one dared say a word to him.

It had been like that for years: no one could say anything to Sasha. No one could teach him anything. He'd get angry, and everyone stayed quiet on account of his temper which descended on the Lurie household like a cloud.

One day Tsilke dressed in her new winter coat.

"Where are you going?" Mrs. Lurie asked her.

"Just going for a walk . . ."

"She's growing into a lady," Mrs. Lurie thought, "She's going for a walk by herself."

But Tsilke was going to look for Sasha. She asked around and found Katowska's Cukiernia. She entered, finding herself in a large smoke-filled room where Sasha and some others stood with long cues, playing in silence.

He did not notice her at first in the fog of smoke. Suddenly he saw her by the door.

Her piercing eyes looked so clear and bright; her gaze so detached from the rest of her, dressed now in new city clothes.

The forest . . .

All of last summer stood before Sasha's eyes, demanding, punishing and imploring . . .

The cue stayed frozen in his hands; the other players turned around.

"That's his wife," one of them said.

"She's come after him."

"Why did he get married, the idiot!"

Sasha ignored their insults. He found himself put on the spot. It was a matter of pride: He did not want to show that he was dependent on someone, that someone held him back from doing what he wanted.

But Tsilke looked with a gaze where pleading struggled with anger, and Sasha did not know what to do in that moment . . . Should he stop playing, or continue to hit the balls?

She stood by the door, scanning the room and turned to Sasha:

"Keep playing, Sasha, I'll watch."

Sasha's steps were heavy; the cue trembled in his hands.

"I'll finish this game tomorrow," he blurted out, putting on his coat.

"Let's go, Tsilke!"

They walked out in silence. She—lost and frightened; he—angry. The further they walked and the longer the silence, the stronger his rage burned.

He snapped at her, saying something that he was to regret instantly:

"Why did you have to butt in? What do you all want from me? What? What?"

She did not respond, but stared wide-eyed. He was saying such words to *her*? He's shouting at *her* like that? She came to a halt not far from Lurie's house, as though frozen to the spot. Not saying a word, not blinking an eye. And a light snow fell slowly on her, on Sasha and on the whole street. It fell gently, almost playfully. In the tranquil forest there used to be snow like this too, and she had liked to stand on the porch listening to the silence of the white forest.

Sasha looked at her; his anger had subsided, and he now felt sympathy for her. Why had he offended her? What fault was it of hers?

"Let's go inside. It's cold, Tsilke."

She did not answer.

"Come on inside, Tsilke!"

She gazed off down the street, not saying a word.

Sasha took her by the arm and led her into the house.

That evening he did not leave her side.

He spoke to her, begging her to forgive him. But she did not respond. He took her hand and squeezed it, but her arm hung limp and lifeless.

Sasha felt that something had changed in her, that her sudden stubbornness was not going to go away so quickly. They had skipped dinner and spent the whole night in their clothes. She fell into an uneasy sleep, while he sat and thought.

It felt as though he had lost her today.

By shouting at her one time as they were coming out of Katowska's Cukiernia . . .

That one offense.

He was filled with regret for everything: his freedom, his independence, his studies, billiards, cards, all his travels and foreign newspapers.

It all seemed so petty, so empty compared to Tsilke's open smile, which she always carried for him in her bright eyes, which he had felt threatened by earlier today, yesterday and the day before.

The fact that Tsilke had become his priority, that responsibility which he had been running from his whole life, did not seem so terrible.

He wanted to wake her up and speak to her, to confess that she was indeed his priority.

But she had fallen asleep, fully dressed, offended and alienated.

Day broke.

Tsilke did not want to come out.

"What's wrong with her? Is she not well? Maybe we should call for a doctor."

With great effort they managed to convince her to eat something, but she refused categorically to sit at the dining table.

They took turns going in to her; old man Lurie, his wife, Hela . . .

Each came with kind words. She did not respond. Like a flower that had stopped blooming, she stopped smiling, stopped enchanting people with her glance.

"Tsilke, what's wrong?"

"Nothing . . ."

"What do you want?"

"Nothing . . ."

And that *nothing* sounded so hopeless, so pained . . .

They went to Sasha:

"Did you offend her somehow?"

"I raised my voice one time, and she got angry."

He did not go back to Katowska's. He hung his head and moped through the rooms in his wealthy house, sullen, unsatisfied.

In the city they were saying:

"That young wife at the Luries. . ."

"Is melancholic . . ."

"And the young master . . ."

"Likes billiards more than he likes his wife, or parents."

Tsilke would stand for hours on end by the window watching the snow fall; how white it shone into the soul. But then she saw how the whiteness was trodden underfoot by passersby.

"What was she thinking during those hours? No one knew, though it pained them. They had grown truly very fond of her, she was like a child to them, and no one is spared by the gloomy shadow that descends when a child is sad.

Old man Lurie joked that the apple didn't fall far from the tree—and Tsilke was starting to resemble her silent father.

But she used to laugh so loud.

And she would ask such naive questions, which everyone laughed so indulgently at.

Now she refused to leave her room, did not want to put on a new dress, and all the jewellery she got, all the gifts, were lying around, abandoned.

Word reached Iser that his daughter was not well and so he came to Grodno. He had not wanted to show his face earlier, because he felt guilty towards the Luries.

Because in the hot summer days his daughter had . . .

Now—he stood before her, saddened by her pale complexion.

"Do you not feel well here, Tsilke? The Luries are fond of you, you know?"

She said nothing; tears rolled down her cheeks.

Iser went back to his silent woods, and the silence enveloped the Luries too.

Sasha hid himself away in another room with his books.

Hela stopped singing and playing the piano.

The parents were angry at their son, and the son was angry with the whole world.

It seemed that if Tsilke would only come out of her room and smile, everything would come back to life.

But she remained silent.

Like a stranger, like a proud princess imprisoned in a tower, the barefoot girl from the forest who had, by chance, fallen in with the wealthy . . .

Her silence continued . . .

9

In Mistebove . . .

IVAN THE ROAD WARDEN often came to visit Aunt Nikhe in Mistebove, where she now lived in Barash's house. There were two large, whitewashed rooms, warm and bright. There were copper utensils that hung on the walls, and pristine bedding.

Iser would visit from Svislotsh every Shabbes to pray and speak with Barash. Iser and Nikhe lived peacefully and quietly in their old age.

And Tsilke was gone.

But the next time Ivan came to Mistebove to visit Nikhe, he saw a familiar pair of eyes which he recognized from all those years ago.

Tsilke . . .

Where had she come from, young Lurie's wife? What was she doing there? And why did she look so pale?

He reached out his hand to her, and she responded with a smile.

"Nikhe," Ivan called out.

"What?"

"What's Tsilke doing here?"

"Shhhh . . ."

The old woman beckoned to Ivan, and they went into the other room together.

"Don't talk, Ivan. Don't scare her."

"What happened?"

"You remember how she once ran away from Grodno. She was just a little girl then, you remember? Well, now she's run away again. She turned up ten days ago, half frozen and mute."

"Ran away? From Grodno, from her husband, from such wealth?"

"Shhh . . ."

Ivan left. He understood that he was in the way.

Indeed ten days previously Tsilke had arrived unannounced. It was night-time, Nikhe opened the door and Tsilke had slunk in like a shadow . . .

"Tsilke!" Aunt Nikhe had called out, thinking it was a dream,

But there she was, standing before her. She threw her arms around Nikhe's neck, kissing her and weeping.

"What happened? Why did you come?"

"I ran away . . . I don't belong there . . . I'm never going back."

"But why?"

"Strange, so strange, everything there became strange to me . . ."

And that was all she would say.

The next day, old man Lurie arrived. He'd come personally to find his son's wife who'd snuck out and ran away.

He explained to Nikhe that Sasha had gone away to St. Petersburg for a short while, on account of his papers and that, before he left, Tsilke and he had exchanged angry words.

And since then she had been silent . . .

Melancholic . . .

She had cast aside all her new clothes and jewellery.

Barely ate . . .

And finally ran away.

Lurie approached Tsilke and spoke to her, imploring her to return with him to Grodno.

"I never want to go back there."

"And what about Sasha? You don't want to see him again?"

Sasha . . .

She became pensive. Such a happy summer it had been, he had lain with her by the stream for nights on end. He'd spoken such tender words to her, he had held her in his arms . . . Those were such precious, radiant days . . . The forest sang deep into their souls . . . That summer.

Now she sat wrapped in her aunt's headscarf, gazing out the window at the low cottages, which appeared to be covered in white blankets, and beyond the cottages she could see the woods and a wide, endless sky . . .

"And Sasha, you don't want to see him again?" Lurie asked her again. She answered: "I don't know, I know nothing, I want nothing . . ."

Then Lurie whispered with Aunt Nikhe in the next room.

Two days later he returned, not alone this time, but with Hela. They both tried to talk Tsilke into coming with them.

"No," she shook her head, the hint of a secret smile on her lips.

Hela explained that a letter had arrived from Sasha saying he would be coming back from St. Petersburg soon. He asked them to keep an eye on Tsilke and to love her, promising that when he gets back he will be a better man, will never offend her again . . .

Lurie left the room, and Tsilke stayed alone with Hela.

"My brother is not a bad man . . ."

"He loves you . . ."

"He'll change . . ."

But the Luries returned to Grodno empty handed . . . Leaving the townsfolk baffled:

"What's going on here?"

"She ran away from Grodno . . ."

"From her husband . . ."

"From such wealth . . ."

They told the story in hushed tones in every house, as though cowering from a sudden thunderstorm, striking in mid-winter over the white roofs . . .

"And the Luries themselves . . . the Luries!"

"They come to her as if to an empress . . ."

"Begging her to come back . . ."

"For her to sit on the throne . . ."

"And she says nothing, doesn't want to answer anyone . . ."

"A strange one, that Tsilke . . ."

"Raised in the woods . . ."

"Doesn't know how good she had it . . ."

They watched Barash's house, where Aunt Nikhe lived, as though it hid some great mystery. But Nikhe kept the door firmly shut and remained aloof from the neighbors.

It was winter. The days were white, the cold sun shone in millions of brilliant sparks. If a drop of moisture happened to thaw, it would freeze immediately and remain there shining toward the sky . . .

News of Tsilke's return soon reached Froyke Barash. He had long ago returned home. His father visited him several times in Volkovysk, before eventually bringing him back to Mistebove.

And he seemed to have grown into manhood . . .

Not once had he gotten drunk since his return . . .

He kept himself to himself, and helped his father.

Now he pricked up his ears, lapping up every last word about Tsilke he could catch.

"Ran away . . ."

"Ha!"

"The foreigner" must have insulted her, that must have been it . . .

Tsilke gradually regained her equilibrium in those two enclosed rooms. Several times she had started to speak with her aunt but always trailed off mid-sentence.

"You know, Aunt, it's so stuffy at the Luries', so stifling in Grodno . . ."

"But, child, they have such wealth, so many rooms."

"No, that's not what I mean! It's suffocating there, I could hardly breath . . . In the forest, when I opened the door, I'd see the woods straight away, I was able to run . . . But in Grodno—open the door and there's another door behind it, and streets full of buildings, all so strange and unfamiliar . . ."

"But why did you run away? You love Sasha, don't you?"

"He's distant. Even that summer in the forest there were times when he would not speak and I felt afraid of him . . ."

Gradually her aunt drew the whole story out of her, about the books Sasha read constantly, the billiards, the time he shouted at her in anger because she had followed him.

"Yes, Aunt, at first it was all so exciting: everyone loved me, gave me new clothes, but Sasha grew further and further away from me . . . I could see it and feel it."

"What will happen now? You're still his wife. If you don't go back it will bring terrible shame on your father. And what will become of you?"

"No, Aunt. Whatever happens, I'm not going back to Grodno."

A silence hung in the room. The winter sun was setting. Occasionally a cart would creak past, a sleigh. Children played in the snow, but the cries and laughter of the children did not cause a racket. The great silence of the forest and fields also lay over the village . . . A crow flew past and croaked a message: that life was cruel, *kraa*!

And that night and death wait for all . . .

Kraa!

In the houses people were lighting fires, wood crackling in the stoves. Feather-plucking season had returned to Mistebove, but every few minutes someone would pause in their work to gossip about Tsilke:

"It wasn't an even match, we should have known better . . . "

"But such wealth . . ."

"When you're in love, wealth and poverty are all the same."

"They say there's no way she's going back..."

"And old Lurie said as he was leaving..."

"That he'd never seen anyone as stubborn in all his days..."

Then they would forget about Tsilke for a while, and go back to plucking feathers and singing songs.

The song slipped outside, occasionally reaching as far as Tsilke's ear... it reminded her of other days, happier times, when she had also been afraid of noise and people.

Now she felt that people were always out to trick her... She wrapped herself tighter in her aunt's headscarf and thought about the forest.

By now, all the trees will have been cut down...

She decided she would wait a while, and then she would visit their old house to see for herself what it looked like now.

Aunt Nikhe sat on the other side of the room, glancing at Tsilke from time to time. Lurie had said that she was melancholic, that she shouldn't be provoked.

Iser came for Shabbes. He'd already heard his daughter had run away from Grodno.

When he learned the news he had mumbled to himself:

"She didn't hold out, the child didn't hold out."

No one understood what he meant. He arrived in time for Shabbes, silent as always. He said a few words to Tsilke to reassure her that he was not angry. Tsilke burst into tears, and Nikhe did not budge from her side.

Several weeks passed. Messengers arrived from Grodno, and left empty handed.

The villagers had begun to get used to the new circumstances.

Some neighbors paid Nikhe a visit, to speak about other matters and catch a glimpse of Tsilke.

Froyke's sisters also came by, and Tsilke was more friendly with them, she spoke with them and even told them about Grodno.

The sisters then reported back what they had heard.

And Froyke listened attentively . . .

He was somehow overcome by a new joy: Tsilke had said herself that she would never go back to Grodno . . .

And when Tsilke said something, she meant it. She was headstrong—all people who live in the forest are headstrong—so his grandfather, the Nikolayevsky soldier, has said.

And Froyke went back to polishing his boots. Whenever he saw Nikhe, he greeted her with a friendly, "Good morning."

He regularly told his sisters:

"Pay Tsilke a visit, she's all alone after all."

And when his sisters returned, Froyke would hover around them, looking them in the eye, itching to get a word out of them.

"She's not melancholic at all, that Tsilke," said one sister.

"She laughed today and told stories about the Luries," said another.

"Old Lurie would sit her on his knee and call her *Kozke*. They were all very fond of her."

"Then why did she run away?" Foyke asked.

His sisters did not know. Tsilke had not told them why she ran away, nor had she said a single word about Sasha.

But her Aunt Nikhe was telling people that Tsilke had not been able to get used to the city ways, and yearned for home.

Soon people could hear Tsilke's singing voice whenever they passed below Nikhe's window.

She was singing; she was alive again.

Nikhe was happy: Tsilke would make a full recovery; she would soon come to her senses and go back to Grodno.

In the meantime more and more girls gathered around Tsilke, drawn by a great curiosity.

When they left, the friends would say:

"She's a different person . . ."

"Paler . . ."

"But even more beautiful than before . . ."

"She's really a strange one, up and ran away from her husband, from such a rich house . . ."

"She'll go back, she will . . ."

"Who knows . . ."

Days passed and great heaps of snow accumulated on the rooftops, shaped by the wind into pyramid-like mounds, rounded on one side. There was so much snow gazing in through the windows that it brightened the insides of the houses. A great, white world hung over the little houses, and over the nearby graveyard.

One pair of large, bright eyes in particular often gazed sadly through the window at the world outside, at the whiteness . . .

Tsilke's eyes . . .

As though they wanted to ask something of the wider world, as though they sought solace.

And she cheered up for the first time when Ivan returned.

She was going to go with him into the forest and take one last look at her old home . . .

"There's not much forest to speak of, Tsilke, the trees are almost all gone, and the three cabins are boarded up and covered in snow."

But she begged Ivan, and her aunt Nikhe. She wanted to see what the stream looked like, and the road.

"Fine!"

But how would she walk in the city shoes she'd brought back from Grodno? The snow was very thick.

"Aunt, where are my father's old boots . . ."

"Child, you're going in boots? You think it's . . ."

But Tsilke was already searching in every corner. She found her father's old boots. But as she was putting them on, her arms fell limp and her heart felt heavy: the boots were so crude and heavy; Grodno had left its mark on her after all . . .

She sighed, angry with herself.

A moment later she was wearing her father's boots, wrapped in her aunt's headscarf and ready to set off with Ivan.

The snow already had that softness that comes with the first warm winds, as they flow in from the south making the air milder. What's more, the sun had opened its wide eye, melting the frost with sharp rays, drilling here and there into the depths, down to the hard earth. The sun licked the firmly packed snow through the holes, until a shingle, a roof tile peaked through.

Tsilke walked by Ivan's side. She opened her eyes wide, and it seemed as if she had not been there for a long, long time. The brightness made her feel like skipping, squealing for joy . . . Who to? To nobody. Who does the bird call to? The crow? Who does the squirrel call to in the summer? Who does the eternal stream babble to?

Ivan looked at her and felt a closeness, an affinity to the girl who'd been born in the very forest where he had lived out his life. He was not surprised that she was the way she was, that she had run away from the Luries: each is drawn to one's own, and Tsilke could not adapt to the big city . . .

Ivan understood it quite well, though he'd believed her love for Sasha Lurie might have kept her there.

He interrupted their silence to ask:

"Do you not miss him, Tsilke?"

"Who?"

"You don't want to see Sasha? Last summer, the two of you were as thick as thieves."

Tsilke considered for a moment. She pictured Sasha: plump with dark, half-sleepy eyes. He was kind, he held her in his arms, and yet he was so distant, so unknown. No, she did not miss him, but there was a terrible pain deep in her heart as if it were being stabbed with a spear.

"Let's not talk about that, Ivan, tell me about the forest instead, what does it look like now?"

"We're almost there, you'll see everything for yourself."

They continued in silence. He looked in one direction, she in the other, and they both saw bare fields decked in white. Here and there a hillock or a lone tree stood out, exposed to the elements.

Tsilke looked into the distance. From this very spot she used to be able to see the forest, the woods which were her home, the Luries' three cabins with the stables, but this time she did not see the forest. And suddenly she stumbled upon the first cadaver of a tree, followed by a second . . . a series of round stumps, half covered in snow, fencing off the flatness of the white path. Peaking out were little seats, the roots of the felled trees. There was a large heap of woodchip and branches that looked like the nest of an enormous animal, and everything was peppered with snow, blanketed in winter.

Just then, Tsilke spotted her house. And as her eyes scanned the surrounding whiteness, she saw the terrible destruction that had been wrought there . . .

The great forest lay stretched out on the earth. Bodies in funeral shrouds stretched out, each one isolated from the next. As though bandits had struck the forest in the night, and run away the next morning, their work unfinished. Here and there terrified groups of trees stood, whole patches unfelled. They stood there with pine needles as lush as ever, seeming to stare with terrified, green eyes at their fallen brothers, at the enormous graveyard, waiting . . .

Ivan set off for home while Tsilke stayed alone.

She turned right, left, she was close, she had already reached the three houses, all three were closed, the windows boarded up with planks . . .

Shhhh . . .

All around was so quiet. A winter bird jabbering on the skeleton of a tree, and on another tree hung a piece of rope—a remnant of Aunt Nikhe's washing-line.

Tsilke's eyes darted to and fro as she crept over the dead, snow-covered trees. And when she got tired she brushed some snow off one of the tree stumps and sat down on it. She sat and looked. There used to be life and warmth in this corner. Even during the worst frosts a plume of blue smoke had risen from the house, pouring out of the chimney, sneaking through the green canopy and drifting high into the sky. All was still, white, and bright all around.

It had never been so bright there before. But the brightness weighed so heavily on Tsilke's heart that she was on the verge of tears. She kicked the frozen snow with her father's boots until the tree revealed its golden bark.

Empty all around . . .

Where were the paths she walked with Sasha?

Where had the gypsies set up camp?

She did not recognize her home . . . and where was the stream?

She climbed down from the stump she'd been sitting on and went to find the stream. It was covered in branches and woodchip, and the frost had forged the branches together into one icy whole.

Everything was different, poorer, emptier. Only light and snow remained. Light and snow. She missed her footing, and realized that she had never felt so lost . . . she had arrived at an unfamiliar forest, a forest being cut down. She looked at the three boarded-up, locked buildings, at the quiet porch of their cabin where she used to sit on summer mornings, greeting the forest . . . She looked and recognized the ruins of her home, and the tears began to flow from her heart to her eyes, where they became stuck, frozen. . .

She set off back home, her spirits low. The heavy boots, her father's boots, grew even heavier; the snow clung to them. She felt exhausted, forlorn.

Not far from Mistebove, she saw her aunt coming toward her.

Nikhe had worried that Tsilke had been gone so long.

"Was it worth it? Tsilke . . . Was it worth dragging yourself all the way out there?"

"They've cut down almost everything, Aunt . . ."

"What of it? It's not the first forest to be chopped down."

"But, my trees, they grew up with me . . ."

"A person is a person, and trees are just wood . . ."

The two women walked home, wrapped in headscarves, barely uttering a word. And as they entered the town they were followed from a discreet distance by Froyke. He did not appear to be watching them. His gaze was directed at the houses covered in snow, at the edge of the sky, which encircled the whole of Mistebove.

Froyke had one thought in his mind, one prayer, one desire:

Don't let her go back to Grodno . . .

Let her stay here among the snow-covered houses.

He felt reborn. He held his head up proudly. So he still has a chance: she'd run away from such wealth in Grodno . . . Why? What was it to him? As long as she was in Mistebove, in the other half of his father's house, right next door where he could hear her singing through the wall.

And Tsilke . . .

Tsilke returned from the forest, upset:

"Our house locked, the windows boarded up with planks."

"And what about this place, Tsilke, it's not such a bad house: it's warm, bright, and clean," Aunt Nikhe danced around her, and when Tsilke had calmed down a little, the conversation moved on:

"You'll go back to your family now soon, won't you Tsilke, back to the Luries?"

Tsilke silently shook her head: "No."

"Why not?"

"He shouted at me. Sasha lost his temper with me, he raised his voice in anger."

Nikhe sat closer to Tsilke:

"Husbands shout sometimes . . . What's the big deal? He loses his temper and then everything goes back to normal . . . What's the big deal?"

Tsilke straightened herself up, stood up and declared with hurt pride:

"Nobody shouts at me . . . He carried me in his arms, didn't leave the forest for weeks . . . Because of me. But in Grodno he started hiding from me, sneaking off into a separate room, playing billiards, I didn't see him for days on end . . . No, Aunt Nikhe! It's over, over . . ."

"What, *over*?"

"I'm not going back there. You need to talk to Father. And if old Lurie comes back you need to talk to him too, you need to tell everyone that Tsilke is never going back to Grodno ever again . . ."

She was upset, tears running from her eyes. Nikhe went to sit in a corner and did not say another word.

Iser came for Shabbes. He arrived with a few half words, said something to Nikhe, mumbled something to Tsilke and sat for the rest of the day with his nose buried in a holy book.

After Havdole he went to Tsilke and looked her deep in the eyes . . .

"Tsilke . . ."

She shivered. She knew her father's visit meant something serious.

"What is it, father?"

"Will you obey everything I tell you to do?"

She hesitated for a moment and said:

"Everything."

He laid his hands on her shoulders and continued:

"Your Sasha is back from St. Petersburg, the Luries are waiting for you, it's not a nice situation . . ."

"What do you want, father?"

"I want you to go back to Grodno tomorrow, I'll come with you . . ."

She sprang to her feet, ran to the window and stood there in silence . . . Until her father spoke again:

"What is it, Tsilke?"

"I won't go . . . There's nothing for me there, no one for me."

Iser tried his last hand:

"If you don't go, I probably won't come back to Mistebove, I'll rot away somewhere in the woods, but I won't come back here. Neither you nor your Aunt Nikhe will ever see me again . . ."

"Father!"

They looked at each other for a moment.

She was the first to speak:

"If you won't come home, and you all continue to torment me about going to Grodno, I know what I'll do."

There was silence. Iser, Nikhe and Tsilke, all three retreated into their own thoughts.

"What will you do?" Iser asked.

"There are still some trees in our old place in the forest, and I'll find a rope somewhere."

Nikhe ran towards her:

"Pfui to that! Starting the new week with such words, shame on you Tsilke, have you lost your mind . . . Pfui to that . . ."

Her gaze darted nervously between Tsilke and Iser.

Aunt Nikhe was all too familiar with stories about ropes on trees.

A few years ago a girl from Mistebove had hanged herself in the woods, on account of some man . . .

Iser stood mute. Terrified. He stared at the wall, at the window. Running his fingers through his beard, he did not say another word.

Later, as he sat with a holy book, he said to Nikhe, loud enough for Tsilke to hear.

"Let her do what she wants, whether she goes or not . . ."

From that day on no one mentioned another word about Grodno or the Luries. The three people who had lived out their lives in the forest, understood each other through half-words, through what was left unsaid. Each was stubborn in their own way, and they hid their anger deep down. Every conflict ended with a long silence . . .

Tsilke often went back to the site of the old forest, to the three boarded up cabins.

The townsfolk began to regard her with a strange respect. When they saw her passing in her aunt's headscarf and father's boots, they would shrug:

"She's off to the forest, the empty almost entirely treeless forest . . ."

"As if she's visiting a grave . . ."

"And she ran away from such wealth . . ."

"Melancholic . . ."

"Just like her old man . . ."

But their respect for her remained intact. Iser the forest warden's daughter, the forest girl everyone knew since she used to walk to Mistebove barefoot as a child. They looked at her now like royalty ...

"One of these days she'll get up and fly off somewhere ..."

"No, she'll go back to Grodno, to that rich family, to the Luries ..."

"Such wealth, such millions!"

"A family with a good name ..."

But she did not go to the Luries. She would visit Ivan the old road watchman, and the mute forest which lay in pieces on the ground. She would exchange a few words with Ivan, and with the forest she would share a long silence, hours of silence.

The further she went from the road, the more trees there were left. And Tsilke liked to wander in the white dense winter forest. On a frosty day, when the vapor of her breath froze immediately, and the trees stood tense like thick cords, like pillars of steel, in the frozen silence you could hear a crackle, a groan, like a clay pot breaking: It was the frost bursting the bark off the trees ...

Suddenly she heard the cat-like squeak of a squirrel. The golden scamp was not frozen, and its squeak carried so far. The sound was not a sad one, but resounded with firm certainty ...

The certainty that there will always be forests.

That the green heads of the trees will always stretch towards the sky.

Often, on her way back, Tsilke saw Aunt Nikhe from afar; Nikhe always worried when Tsilke tarried too long. The old woman seemed to bring warmth for Tsilke, who had been frozen to the bones out in the woods, and there was food waiting for her at home.

Whenever Nikhe noticed that Tsilke was bored, she would go next door and invite the Barash girls over, and they would invite other girls.

They gladly visited Tsilke. She had been to Grodno after all, and she was so pretty that even a foreigner had fallen in love with her.

A strange character: running away from money—yes, the girls were happy to pay Tsilke a visit . . .

One thing led to another until eventually Froyke ventured into Iser's house. At first he came to call on his sisters. The second time he found a new excuse. Tsilke watched him curiously each time. She remembered, had no choice but to remember . . . The time in the sled when he was kissing the girls and he had wanted to kiss Tsilke too, but she had been afraid of him. Now she was no longer afraid . . . She also recalled how he had danced with the gypsy woman in the forest, and how Tsilke's heart had begun to pound . . . Since then she had dreamed of him often . . .

Froyke with his boots—he was calmer now, his shoulders had grown broad, and he sought out Tsilke with his eyes. It seemed as though he was always on the verge of telling her something. But they were never alone together. Aunt Nikhe did not leave the room for a second, and Tsilke's friends were always sitting there, chatting and laughing.

One time Tsilke said that if Froyke wanted . . .

"What?" several girls asked in unison.

"If he set up the sled and we went off over the fields . . ."

Froyke's sisters burst into laughter. The other girls laughed too. And Froyke blushed. Tsilke did not understand why they were laughing, or why Froyke had gone red. She did not know that months ago Froyke had set off for Volkovysk with his horse and drank it all away.

And all because of Tsilke. Because she had married the "foreigner."

One of Froyke's sisters said:

"We don't have a horse anymore—long since sold!" But they did not say why, for fear of embarrassing Froyke.

And because he was calm . . .

And because he would stare at her with such devotion in his eyes, Tsilke also began to look at him more.

And she spoke to her Aunt with an open heart:

"You know, Aunt, I feel happier when Froyke comes to visit."

Nikhe opened her old eyes . . .

"Who, Froyke? Do you reckon he'll ever make something of himself?"

"What does that even mean, *make something of himself,* Aunt!"

"It means being a decent person, living like a decent person . . ."

"And Froyke doesn't live like a decent person?" He's not a decent person?"

The old woman was confounded by Tsilke's questioning, and went back to her pots in a huff.

Froyke came by every day now, except Shabbes, when Iser was home. He was afraid of the old man.

He would stand by the oven, warming himself. He grew ever more bold and cheerful. And Nikhe mumbled to herself:

"They have their own oven . . . Why does he come here?"

"He comes to see Tsilke."

"And she's glad he comes."

"She watches him, laughs when he laughs, sings when he sings."

"Like cats, they're courting each other."

The dishes fell from Nikhe's hands as they had that summer when Sasha was staying in the forest.

How much she had already suffered, Aunt Nikhe. How many sleepless nights on account of the motherless child, and she always thought that everything was her fault. She would be punished for it. She had grown grayer and bent, she who'd lived her best years in solitude. She'd had only one celebration in her life, one consolation: putting on a new wig, and reading Bible stories.

Now that Froyke was becoming a regular guest, and Tsilke was happy that he came, Nikhe no longer knew what to do.

Iser returned to Mistebove; he paid no attention to anyone, least of all Tsilke.

Nikhe had no desire to talk to strangers about it. Talk to Tsilke herself? She needed to come to terms with the reality that she had a husband in Grodno, she needed to put aside her whims and go back to the Luries. In every town and village people were gossiping about it. About the poor girl who married a Lurie only to run away a few months after the wedding for no reason at all.

But Tsilke was strong-willed, and no amount of words were going to make any difference.

So Nikhe held her tongue, and sighed . . .

And there was nothing she could do when Froyke turned up one night with a sled. He had borrowed it from a neighbor, a Christian. He pulled up outside and called out to Tsilke . . .

"How about a sleigh-ride?"

At night alone: Tsilke, a married woman who'd run away from her husband . . . With Froyke the sausage-eater! Nikhe wanted to block the doorway, to stop Tsilke from going out. But Tsilke did not even look at her aunt. She slipped past, wrapped in a headscarf.

A white night. The horse broke into a steady trot—and the houses with their fires disappeared behind them. The fields began, open fields under the starry sky. The snow, which had melted slightly in the light of day, now broke like glass under the horse's hooves. The sled flew over low hillocks, and shallow troughs . . .

Tsilke accidentally fell against Froyke's shoulders several times, and she found herself hoping the sled would shake again so that she could fall against him once more.

With each shake, Froyke opened his mouth and laughed, laughed to Tsilke and into the night.

But what had happened to his former audacity?

He would long ago have let go of the reins and his hands would have been busy with something else, but he was still afraid of Tsilke. He looked her in the eye, counting and weighing up her every word . . .

Had she already forgotten about that Lurie?

And does she like him, Froyke?

When the sled began to swim slowly over the snow they spoke about various things, but very little about themselves.

Tsilke said that at the Luries' place in Grodno there was a box, like the nobleman had in Prudne: They called it a *fortepiano*, and Tsilke liked to run her fingers over it, making such strange sounds, sounds that reminded her somehow of the forest.

She told him about old Lurie, who would sit her on his knee.

She told him all sorts of details about everyone, but she never once mentioned Sasha's name.

This surprised Froyke, but he did not want to ask about it.

"Froyke!" Tsilke called out suddenly.

"Yes?"

"When summer comes, let's go together through the woods, around here, in the parts that haven't been cut down. I'll go barefoot, and you'll wear your shiny boots like you did with your gypsy woman . . . Do you remember?

She looked him boldly in the eyes . . . Any minute now he'd let go of the reins, any minute . . . But the lights of Mistebove were glinting up ahead; they were already home.

Tsilke ran into the house, the frost playing on her face. She looked around; her aunt was in bed, asleep, or pretending to be. The old woman had already made Tsilke's warm bed with her thin hands . . . Tsilke threw herself onto the bed and closed her eyes. The blood coursed quickly through her veins. Her heart pounded, and fragmentary images floated in her mind's eye . . . The forest, the road, Froyke and the gypsy, Sasha and Grodno, old Lurie. But she wanted to disentangle all these images, because her hands were drawn to one figure, to Froyke.

Such round shoulders he had. Part of his chest was exposed, covered in thick, black hair . . . And it seemed as though, at any moment, he would grab her by the hand and run away with her. And if he did not want to, she would grab him herself and run, run with him to the stream, to the twin pines and further still.

Suddenly she opened her eyes. She was surprised not to find Froyke by her side, but instead of Froyke, she saw Aunt Nikhe, sitting on her bed looking at her, watching her every movement. Old and bent, cranky and kind at the same time, she gazed at Tsilke with the look of another world. Tsilke was not surprised to see her staring at her . . .

Her aunt had every right to stare . . .

And Tsilke's heart, pounding so fast, had every right to pound . . .

Both women stared at each other. Tsilke was the first to look away. She shook out her hair, and hid under the blanket.

The next morning, Froyke's sisters came by and Tsilke told them about the previous night's sleigh-ride. The sleigh had shaken and the snow had shattered like shards of clay. Then when she'd got home, her face had stung from the cold and she had slept like a baby.

Froyke's sisters told the neighbors that Tsilke was happier and in better spirits, and in the town there were already insinuations that Froyke had fulfilled his conquest...

"And what will Grodno have to say about it?"

"Ah, the big-shots, you can never tell with them."

In Mistebove there was no shortage of girls carrying out love affairs, but Tsilke and Froyke were the favored topic of discussion.

When paying visits to the Barashes, or to other neighbors, Tsilke herself had now become a little reserved, a little shy. People liked her and their curiosity about her knew no bounds...

"She's different somehow..."

"Grew up in the woods."

"But, Froyke..."

"When someone catches his eye..."

"Even the Luries' millions won't help..."

It was now Purim. Snow fell and snow melted. The sun would warm up half a rooftop, melting the snow, while the other half was still shrouded in white... Outside the town the waters were already beginning to flow, snow mingling with the softened earth. It was no longer possible for Tsilke to walk in the forest, it was hard to walk even in her father's boots. A breeze would blow from the woodlands, bringing the scent of freshly cut wood, and the smell of last years leaves and pine-needles.

Ivan paid Nikhe a visit. He had been to St.Petersburg for several weeks where his son was serving in the army. He said it was very hard for him in the big city.

"There was a lot to see, but I was confused, so in the end I didn't see anything. I'm a simple man, I need to see the sky several times a day; it stretches out so wide here over our road . . . The forest is a better place for the likes of me."

Tsilke took up his last words:

"Exactly right, Ivan! The forest is better for people like us. When summer comes, I'm going to go with Froyke into what's left of the woods . . ."

"With Froyke?" Ivan asked with wide-eyed curiosity.

Tsilke was embarrassed.

She had not yet had time to take stock of everything she'd been feeling these last days. The joy she felt when Froyke spoke. And now Ivan from the forest was asking out loud: *With Froyke?*

Ivan came closer and laughed in her face:

"With Froyke it is then. You'll come to the forest and I'll show you what a beautiful fox I caught; I have him in a cage."

Then Ivan went to talk to Nikhe in the next room, about domestic things, like one of the family.

Iser did not come to Mistebove the next Shabbes. He told someone in Svislotsh that he would have to stay in the forest that week.

Froyke more than anyone was delighted to hear the news. A whole Shabbes without that hot-tempered mute, Iser!

Minding her own business, Aunt Nikhe said nothing, save for the occasional disapproving mumble, as Froyke sat next to Tsilke.

The aunt he could handle, let her be as angry as she wanted.

It was Friday evening, after the blessing of the candles. The men were praying. Twice Tsilke asked Froyke why he had not gone to pray with the others. Froyke stood there calmly next to Ivan, warming himself by the stove and smiling:

"Praying? I'll have plenty of time to pray when I'm old."

The candles burned. A tranquility came in from the dark street outside. Tsilke stood next to the stove too . . . Aunt Nikhe was reading a siddur, firing evil looks at the pair every few minutes.

Froyke's hand roamed by the warm stove, until it found one of Tsilke's fingers . . .

Just one finger . . .

And he felt as though he had conquered the world, he had defeated a wealthy man, because Tsilke did not take her finger away. He squeezed it in his firm hand, played with it . . . And he felt as though the whole of Tsilke—she who used to proudly reject his advances, who married another man before running away—that Tsilke was as subservient to him now as her little finger, which warmed itself in his hand.

Later, when Nikhe had disappeared for a moment next door, Froyke looked at Tsilke, and Tsilke looked at Froyke . . .

He took a step away from the stove, gently leading her. Instead of one finger he now held both her hands. He looked at her with burning eyes for a moment . . .

And they fell upon each other. He bit into her lip, and she closed her eyes from the pain. It felt as though a song rang out throughout the whole house, the whole world, and their hearts . . .

And afterwards she realized that Froyke was trying to say something to her, practically shouting:

"Write to him, tell him you want a divorce . . ."

The door opened. They heard footsteps—Aunt Nikhe had come back and Froyke met her in the doorway:

"I'm off to pray, Nikhe!"

The old woman glared in astonishment:

"So religious all of a sudden?"

Froyke was gone. Nikhe looked at Tsilke who stood lost in thought, with a half-smile on her lips. And when her aunt called out:

"Tsilke!"

She trembled; the light shudder caused her hair to come undone, and it flowed over her shoulders like a stream of gold.

GLOSSARY

Arendar [ארענדאר]
A lease-holder of a farm, estate or property. There was a long tradition of Polish nobility leasing estates or businesses to Jewish *arendars*, particularly taverns, inns, lumber mills etc.

Cukernia
A bakery and café serving a variety of pastries.

Gabbai [גבאי/*gabe*]
A person who assists in running a synagogue.

Gymnasium
A secondary school preparing students for higher education at a university.

Havdole [הבדלה]
Ceremony marking the end of *Shabes* where blessings are made over wine.

Kaddish [קדיש/*kadesh*]
The Mourner's Kaddish", said as part of the mourning rituals in Judaism in all prayer services, as well as at funerals and memorials.

Karahod (קאַראַהאָד)

Traditional circle dance.

Lithuania (ליטע/*lite*)

Here, an area much larger than the modern state of Lithuania. Homeland of the Litvaks, a group whose regional identity is considerably older and more stable than the borders of Eastern Europe, living in the area roughly equivalent to modern-day Lithuania, Latvia, Belarus and parts of north-east Poland. The Litvaks differed from the *Poylish* (Polish) Jews and *Galitsyaner* (Galician/Ukrainian) Jews in their dialect, cuisine, and temperament.

Nikolayevsky Soldier

Jews drafted into Russian military service from 1827 to 1856. Named for Nicholas I (1825–1855) whose *Ustav rekrutskoi povinnosti* (Statute on Conscription Duty) marked the beginning of compulsory military service for Jewish males over the age of 18. Military service lasted a staggering 25 years after which many Jews had all but abandoned much of their Jewish identity.

Reb (רב)

Yiddish honorific, equivalent to Mr. Used with full name, or first name only.

Shabes (שבת)

Judaism's day of rest on the seventh day of the week, ie. Saturday.

Shammes [שמש/*shames*]

The caretaker of a synagogue. Often translated as beadle or sexton.

Siddur [סידור/*sider*]

Prayer book containing the essential prayers used throughout the year.

Starosta

An elected community elder and administrator.

Sukkes [סוכות/*sukes*]

Also known as the Feast of Tabernacles. An eight day festival, beginning and ending with holy days. The festival is traditionally celebrated by building an outdoor hut, known as a Sukkah, the walls and roof of which are covered in *skhakh* (palm leaves or nearest available equivalent) where families eat their meals and sometimes sleep.

Tefilin [תּפֿילין/*tfiln*]

Tefillin, often called phylacteries, are small leather boxes containing tiny scrolls of parchment, worn during morning prayer, on the forehead and arm, secured by leather straps.

Uriadnik

A low-ranking district policeman in Tsarist Russia.

Acknowledgements

Special thanks to Mindl Cohen, Saul Noam Zaritt, Eliezer Niborski, Ze'ev Duckworth, Jessica Kirzane, and Olivia Oldham.

Zusman Segalovitsh

Born in Białystok into a middle-class family with a rabbinical background, Segalovitsh (1884–1949) received both a traditional Jewish and modern secular education. Living variously in Łódź, Odessa, Crimea, the Caucuses, Kiev and Moscow, he eventually settled in Warsaw, where he was one of the leading figures in the city's literary establishment during the interwar period. A prolific writer of both poetry and prose, Segalovitsh achieved considerable success through his novels which were runaway bestsellers.

Segalovitsh fled Warsaw in 1939 and made his way over land to Palestine, settling in Tel-Aviv where he lived for the next seven years. While there he wrote three major works of autobiography including Tlomackie 13, a tribute to the Yiddish Writer's Union in Warsaw.

He died suddenly in 1952 while travelling in New York

Segalovitch in English Translation

They Are No More, trans. Amelia Levy. Ophir / The Jewish Arts Association of South Africa, 1949.

Daniel Kennedy is a translator based in France. His translations include:

Hersh Dovid Nomberg

Warsaw Stories, White Goat Press, 2019.

A Cheerful Soul and Other Stories, Snuggly Books, 2021.

Happiness and Other Fictions, Snuggly Books, 2022.

Zalman Shneour

A Death: Notes of a Suicide, Wakefield Press, 2019.

Isaac Bashevis Singer

Shammai Weitz, Sublunary Editions, 2022.

FARLAG

Farlag Press is an independent publisher run by a collective of translators and literature-lovers. We prioritise translations from stateless and minority languages, as well as the writings of exiles, immigrants and other outsiders.

We are a strictly for-loss company, though we are registered as a non-profit association in France.

www.farlag.com

Also Available

1. Moyshe Nadir *Messiah in America (A Drama in Five Acts)*
Translated by Michael Shapiro
144pp ISBN: 9791096677047

2. Miriam Karpilove *Judith: A Tale of Love & Woe*
Translated by Jessica Kirzane
146pp ISBN: 9791096677108

Forthcoming titles:

Anna Margolin *During Sleepless Nights and Other Stories*
Translated by Daniel Kennedy

Sam Liptzin *She Sold Her Husband and Other Satirical Sketches*
Translated by Zeke Levine

Farlag Bilingual Series:

1. Hersh Dovid Nomberg *À qui la faute ?* װער איז שולדיק
[Édition bilingue: yiddish/français]
Traduit par Fleur Kuhn-Kennedy
66pp ISBN: 9791096677085

2. Hersh Dovid Nomberg *Between Parents* צװישן טאַטע־מאַמע
[Bilingual edition: Yiddish/English]
Translated by Ollie Elkus and Daniel Kennedy
74pp ISBN: 9791096677092

Ingram Content Group UK Ltd.
Milton Keynes UK
UKHW042024090323
418309UK00001B/248